IN THE CLAWS OF THE CAT

PROSE SERIES 77

Canada Council for the Arts
Conseil des Arts du Canada

ONTARIO ARTS COUNCIL
CONSEIL DES ARTS DE L'ONTARIO

Guernica Editions Inc. acknowledges the support of the Canada Council for the Arts.
Guernica Editions Inc. acknowledges the support of the Ontario Arts Council.

CLAUDE FORAND

IN THE CLAWS OF THE CAT

TRANSLATED BY JO-ANNE ELDER

GUERNICA
TORONTO•BUFFALO•CHICAGO•LANCASTER (U.K.)
2006

Antonio D'Alfonso, editor
Guernica Editions Inc.
PO Box 117, Station P, Toronto (ON), Canada M5S 2S6
2250 Military Road, Tonawanda, N.Y. 14150-6000 U.S.A.

Distributors:
University of Toronto Press Distribution,
5201 Dufferin Street, Toronto (ON), Canada M3H 5T8
Gazelle Book Services, White Cross Mills, High Town,
Lancaster LA1 4XS U.K.
Independent Publishers Group,
814 N. Franklin Street, Chicago, Il. 60610 U.S.A.
First edition.
Printed in Canada.
Legal Deposit – Third Quarter
National Library of Canada
Library of Congress Catalog Card Number: 2006929265
Library and Archives Canada Cataloguing in Publication
Forand, Claude, 1954-
[Cri du chat. English]
In the claws of the cat
Claude Forand ; translated by Jo-Anne Elder.
(Prose series ; 77)
Translation of: Le cri du chat.
ISBN 1-55071-258-6
I. Elder, Jo-Anne II. Title. III. Series.
PS8561.O6335C7413 2006 C843'.54 C2006-903548-2

IN THE CLAWS OF THE CAT

Chapter 1

Joseph Albert Bussières pushed the heavy grilled gate of the Notre Dame cemetery in Chesterville. Walking with a rather nervous step, he cast a quick glance at his watch. It was past eleven p.m. He'd better hurry. The damned rain hadn't let up all night. He made his way onto the main pathway and passed a row of tombstones standing as straight and stiff as sentry guards. The rain and the wind beat against his face. J.A. Bussières turned up the collar of his raincoat. He lit a cigarillo to calm his nerves, but, a moment later, tossed it down like a wet firecracker.

Above his head, the few lamp posts around the cemetery cringed under the downpour and spread only a pale light over the sinister landscape. He raised his eyes. Even the crescent moon was now nearly completely shaded by thick clouds. Around him, funeral monuments slipped away, one by one, into the fog that blanketed the cemetery. Bussières was soaked to his bones and the wet night seemed to be taking great delight in a chance to irritate his rheumatism. He swore, noticing that his Italian leather shoes were soaked too. The damp soil smelled vile enough to make him want to throw up. Goddam land of the dead! During rainstorms, it was as if the tombs opened up so that the Maccabees rotting under his feet could breathe. He shook these stupid thoughts from his head by leaving the main path and wandering silently among the grave stones. Suddenly, he stopped short and turned his ear. It wasn't the rain. Nor was it the wind. Nor his footsteps in the grass. It was something else. It sounded like a scream, a screech.

He abruptly turned around. Someone was following him; he was sure of it. He rushed anxiously towards the main path. The strange sound now seemed to stick under his feet. It seemed to come from behind one of the gravestones. Bussières wanted to find out for sure. Cautiously, he went over. A large black cat leaning up against the stone let out a loud meow when it saw him, and slinked between his legs.

"You gave me a hell of a fright!" He exclaimed, breathing a sigh of relief.

He hated cats. As a child, he had caught a neighbour's kitten and tried to play with it. The animal panicked and scratched his forearm hard enough to leave a deep scar you could still see to this day.

The rain had almost stopped. Only the sound of his footsteps hammering the asphalt of the main path disturbed the silence. All of a sudden, he noticed a human silhouette sitting on a tombstone a few metres in front of him. He went towards it, but the shadowy figure seemed to disappear into the fog covering the cemetery.

"Who's there?" Bussières asked, his voice muted by nerves.

A long meow was the reply. Followed by another.

"I know there's someone there!"

He approached timidly, bolstering himself up by holding on to the tombstones. The territory became more and more familiar. He could make out the monument of his own family, the Bussières plot. This was where his father, mother and two sisters were buried. And this was where his wife, his son and he would some day be put into the earth. Near the superb granite monument his family had constructed thirty years ago, on the most beautiful plot in the parish cemetery, under the century-old maple trees. The fog seemed to waltz in front of his eyes. When it faded, a moment later, he was terrified to see a black shadow less than a metre in front of him. He could make out the glint of a knife blade that leapt up into the air before plunging into his chest once, and then again. Around the corpse of J.A. Bussières, the screeches of a cat now filled the night.

★

The annoying hum of the percolator warned Roméo Dubuc, Chief of Police for the town of Chesterville, that breakfast time had arrived. He sipped a mouthful of black coffee, pulled on his shirt and sat down at the table to eat his three eggs, sunny side up, and some bacon cooked to a crisp. It was a ritual that he had allowed himself four mornings every week for nearly thirty years now – eating habits to which his generous girth could testify. That morning, however, something out of the ordinary was about to take place. Someone was knocking at the door.

"It's open!"

His deputy, Lucien Langlois, wasn't even in uniform. He was a thin, dry man, short, efficient. He gesticulated wildly, without managing to make a single word come out of his mouth.

"Cripes, Lucien! Stop carrying on like that! You look like you've seen a ghost. Why are you waving your arms about?"

The other man remained mute, but Dubuc could tell immediately that something odd had happened. He grabbed his vest and cap, caught two slices of toast in mid-air as they flew out of the toaster, and followed his deputy to the patrol car. It was only once he was behind the steering wheel that Lucien's tongue finally got itself loose.

"It's J.A. Bussières!"

Roméo Dubuc watched him drop syllables, one by one, as he continued to munch on the breakfast that had been interrupted.

"What about him?"

"He's just been found dead!"

Roméo Dubuc felt as though a cannonball had torn through his stomach.

"Dead? How? Come on, out with it!"

"It was Toto Grimaldi who found him, this morning, at the cemetery, when he got to work. Knifed. Disfigured. Toto called me. I came to get you as soon as I could."

Soon, they arrived at the parish cemetery. In a town with a population of only 5,000, where news made its way around the place at supersonic speed, they weren't surprised to see a dozen curious people gathered around the entry gate. Roméo Dubuc waved them aside impatiently, dispersing them so that he could make his way towards the main path.

He arrived close to the spot where the body was lying. The soaked man was lying on his back in a pool of blood, arms spread apart and legs slightly bent. The police officer knelt down next to him. The victim had been stabbed twice in the chest, and his face was horribly mutilated and bloody.

"Not a pretty sight," said Dubuc, turning his head.

Repulsion could be read in the features of both policemen's faces, wracked by the horror of the drama that had hit the little community.

"He looks like he's been scratched. Maybe a raccoon or a hungry rodent?" remarked Lucien.

"Or a murderer," added Dubuc. "Have you called the coroner?"

"Dr. Moreau is on his way, with an ambulance."

Dubuc touched the cold face of the victim.

"If we judge by how stiff the corpse is, the death must have occurred somewhere around seven hours ago. Nine, maybe. But Moreau will be able to confirm that."

He leaned over to look at the wounds more closely.

"Did you see the stab wounds, Lucien? Look at this."

The deputy knelt down beside the body.

"Two deep wounds, very clean. One! Two! The blade must have been plunged right into the heart. Bussières was killed on the spot. No doubt about it. A nice job. Someone who knew how to use a knife, that's for sure. We'll have to see what comes out in the autopsy report."

"No sign of struggle. That's odd," commented Lucien. "It's as if Bussières let himself get stabbed and roughed up without even blinking."

Roméo Dubuc got up to look around the scene.

"The rain last night has completely washed away everything. Too bad; we won't find any tracks in the grass."

Lucien's attention was drawn to the victim's feet.

"Did you notice that? J.A. didn't have any shoes on!"

"I did see that, as soon as I arrived," replied Dubuc. "Maybe he lost them in the grass."

They inspected the surrounding area, but found nothing.

"It's pretty weird, isn't it? You said that Toto Grimaldi was the one who found the body, right? Where is he, anyway?"

"He's shut himself up in the shed at the other end of the cemetery. Waiting for someone to come and get him. Come on, I'll take you over."

Antonio Grimaldi approached them at a snail's pace, visibly reluctant to get anywhere near his macabre discovery. He was in his fifties, a mild-mannered man, and the events of the last few hours had wound his nerves to a ball.

"Come here, Toto. One more Maccabee won't hurt you. You bury corpses by the ton!" Dubuc said, attempted to be jovial.

"That's just it," the other man replied. "When I got to work today I practically tripped over Bussières's body.

There can't be a more awful way to start your day's work, you know."

"Did you notice anything odd?"

"Like what?"

"I dunno. Vandalism, whatever."

He took a second to think, turning his cap around in his rough hands.

"Well, let's see. Nuthin' broke in the cemetery, if that's what you mean."

Chief Dubuc dismissed him, then crouched down again near J.A. Bussières's body to begin the search. His hand met a thick wallet.

He whistled and turned to his deputy.

"Cripes, Lucien, looky here! What a wad of dough! Our friend must have been walking around with half the moolah in Chesterville in his pocket!"

As well as the wallet, a search of the victim's vest pocket yielded a key chain with several keys, a Rolex watch, a package of cigarillos that was nearly empty, a small box of matches, some small change, a gold chain with a charm, as well as a little leather case and some business cards.

"Bussières had at least $5,400 cash on him. Not counting his watch. Do you know how much his famous Rolex watch is worth, Lucien?"

The deputy shrugged.

"I dunno. Maybe a hundred bucks?"

"I said Rolex, my friend, not Timex! Bussières made a point of strutting around showing it off to everyone in the county. It was worth $15,000, what with the diamonds. I know more than one son of a gun in Chesterville who'd be ready to push his mothers off a bridge for that kind of thing."

"And yet it's all still there," the deputy said.

"That's what gets me. J.A. was the biggest big shot in the county and no one touched a thing. Except his shoes."

In order to get the huge ring off the victim's finger, Lucien had to carefully unclench his hand. His fist was clasped around a wildflower.

"Look at this!"

Puzzled, Roméo Dubuc stared at the faded flower clutched in Bussières's hand. Nearby, he found the same variety on a mound of earth close to the corpse.

Footsteps could be heard along the main path, just behind them. It was the coroner, Ernest Moreau, followed by two ambulance attendants. The old country doctor confirmed the death with the matter-of-fact air of one used to looking the Grim Reaper in the eye.

"At first glance, I would suspect that the cause of death was stabbing by a sharp object, such as the blade of a knife. Meanwhile, you can . . . "

He didn't have a chance to finish his sentence. The hammer of high heels down the main path reached them, followed by an uproar difficult to describe. The widow of J.A. Bussières, followed by her chauffeur and a group of hangers-on, made a theatrical entrance. Ignoring the policemen and the doctor, she dissolved into tears at the sight of her husband's body and fell on the body, unconsolable. Behind her, the chauffeur and the ambulance attendants tried desperately to lift her up.

Chief Dubuc asked Lucien to protect the scene of the crime from the curious public, and then went off. As he walked, he noticed a brown object, long and narrow, in the grass. It was a cigarillo, still wet. He rolled it between his fingers and smelled it with visible pleasure.

"Hummmm. I only know one guy in the whole region that smokes cigarillos imported from Cuba, and that was J.A. Bussières."

*

Back at the police station, Roméo Dubuc spent the rest of the morning on the phone, trying to retrace the victim's comings and goings on the day of the murder. At around one in the afternoon, he gathered his notes together and called Lucien into his office.

"I've learned a bit more about our dear millionaire. Bussières got up yesterday morning at about seven o'clock, got washed and dressed, and his chauffeur, Roland Fafard, drove him to church, as he did every morning, so he could attend eight o'clock Mass. Father Bourget even told me that he had taken Communion! Bussières might have been the biggest bastard in the county, but he still came off looking like a model Christian. Anyway at about nine, his chauffeur took him straight to his galvanized steel plant, where he spent the whole morning. At noon, he ate at work and discussed a big contract with some clients from Montréal. His chauffeur came to get him at five o'clock and took him straight home. So far, everything is fine; life is good. It's afterwards that everything got complicated."

"How so?"

"Fafard told me that at around eight o'clock, J.A. asked to be driven to the west end of Chesterville. I've got the notes right here – he went to the corner of Baril and Deguise, to be exact. And he told his chauffeur not to wait for him."

"That's a pretty remote place. Usually deserted. Did Bussières go there often?"

"According to Fafard, it was rare. Since the brutal strike at his plant two years ago, Bussières didn't go anywhere alone. He lived in constant fear that one of his employees would come after him. People have been attacked for less.

The louse locked them out for six months because the union wanted fifty-five cents an hour more."

"Pretty strange. You're right."

"What I don't get, Lucien, is how a guy who has a limousine with a private chauffeur and bodyguard could end up alone in a graveyard at midnight. Morever, in the rain. It's beyond me! I can't for the life of me figure out why Bussières was hanging around a cemetery."

The deputy shrugged.

"Did you talk to his wife?"

"Marguerita? Her lips are sealed. The poor woman has nerves like a pin cushion. We're not going to get anything out of her, for the time being. As for Fafard, he told me everything he knew leading up to the disappearance. I believe his story."

"And no one saw Bussières between eight p.m. and the time of his death?"

"Nobody. I called all around. I checked at his factory, GalvaTech, at the Hotel LaSalle, at the Crocodile tavern, at the Greluche bar, at Ginette's Diner, at the bowling alley, at the pool hall run by the Knights of Columbus. Nothing! Nyet! Zero! It's as if Bussières turned into a pumpkin and stayed that way for four or five hours last night."

"And then turned up again, murdered? Look, that doesn't make sense. He must have been seen somewhere. Chesterville is only as big as the palm of my hand. It's not like it's Montréal. We'll have to go back to the drawing board."

Resigned, Roméo Dubuc slumped down into his chair, crossed his arms behind his head and stretched out his feet. When he got into this position, his deputy could almost hear the gray matter of his brain cells grating against each other.

Footsteps clattered down the stairway leading to the

basement of the police station. The door opened noisily. Jeannot Lejeune, the hot-headed reporter from the *Clarion Express* came in, panting. He was well over forty, but his dashing manner and his square jar made him look like an eternal punk rocker. A look that was reinforced by his black leather jacket and a rebellious tuft of hair that fell onto his forehead.

"Golly, officers, you've disappointed me! Not in a hundred years would you have thought of telling me there was a murder in a cemetery, I guess. I was the last to find out. It looks like you're doing everything you can think of to make my life miserable."

Dubuc suppressed a small yawn.

"What's wrong, Jeannot? Isn't your radio working?"

"You know damned well it wasn't on the police band!" Lejeune shouted, barely able to contain his rage.

The reporter gave himself a slap on the cheek, as if the tragedy was a wake-up call.

"J.A. Bussières! That guy was the pillar of the economy in Chesterville. I spoke to him no more than a couple of days ago. His factory, and his apartment buildings, and his . . . "

"And everyone's nerves, Johnny boy! Think!" ordered Dubuc, standing up and towering over him. "No point getting everyone worked up about it. Women and children first. You know as well as I do that Bussières died of suspicious causes and . . . "

"Suspicious? Well, I guess! Stabbed to death and his face kneaded like pizza dough. I hope you have a suspect, and a good one."

Roméo Dubuc shrugged his shoulders.

"Be a good boy and let us do our job, all right? I can't spit out the names of suspects. You know that."

"Bingo! Another great investigation by our local police

department. It'll end up in the bottom of the desk drawer like the others. You're starting to look pretty bad. Turn up the heat, Chief! This isn't some little robbery in a basement. It's the gruesome murder of the biggest businessman in Chesterville!"

The policeman cast a nasty gaze in Lucien's direction, letting him know he'd had enough of the reporter's cut-rate sermons. The deputy decided it was time to step in.

"Listen, Jeannot, all we know is that J.A. was killed last night in the cemetery, and that he was probably alone. As for the rest, well, you know as much as we do."

The more conciliatory tone of Langlois seemed to defuse the reporter's temper before it could explode with the power of a Hiroshima's bomb.

"Yeah, I believe you. But watch out! I'm going to investigate on my end too, and I intend to keep the readers of the *Clarion* informed."

A laugh from deep in Roméo Dubuc's gut abruptly tore through the room.

"Your professionalism astounds me, Jeannot. I'm sure that people who read your rag won't want to miss a single line of your investigation, Inspector Columbo!"

"Laugh as hard as you like, Chief Dubuc. But if it weren't for my rag, as you call it, the people of Chesterville would be about as well taken care of as Christmas trees in July, as far as our police force is concerned. We'll be in touch. Ciao!"

He slammed the door and disappeared the way he had come in, leaving the two police officers more amused than shocked.

Dubuc tried to pick up the train of his thoughts.

"I may have neglected to check one little thing about Bussières. A single, minor detail."

Lucien looked at him, speechless.

"J.A. was a real skirt chaser. He couldn't keep his hands – or anything else – to himself, if you know what I mean. He was a ladies' man of the worst sort, who had a whole bunch of mistresses around the area. I'm not making it up, Lucien, you know as well as I do. Young beauties, most of them, that he wooed with jewelry and expensive dates."

"You think he could have been with a lady friend the night of his death?"

"Why not? Anyway, that might explain why he wasn't seen all evening. My gut tells me that Bussières may have been the victim of a crime of passion. An old mistress or a husband who'd been cheated on, looking for revenge. That kind of rage would explain why he was mangled but not robbed."

Lucien shrugged and hurried into the next room. He came back with the bag containing the victim's personal belongings, emptied the contents onto the table and took out a small package of matches that he displayed with satisfaction.

"When you mentioned sex, I thought about the matches from Motel Roger that we found in the pocket of Bussières's raincoat."

"Motel Roger!" exclaimed Dubuc. "I should have thought of that before! It's nothing more than a legal whorehouse. They sell tail there cheaper than baloney! Maybe we have a lead. Let's go!"

They hurried straight to the motel, located near the west exit of Chesterville. Motel Roger was a hole in the wall, nondescript and identical to dozens of others along the old highways in the province. But on this day at the end of July, hot and humid, the stagnant water in the pool hadn't attracted any swimmers daring enough to dive in. The place was deserted.

They went up to the front desk. The owner's wife, her

nose in a yellowed copy of *Reader's Digest*, didn't blink an eyelash when they walked in. Roméo Dubuc hammered on the bell that was nearly encrusted in the countertop. The poor woman leapt up and clutched a hand to her generous bosom.

"Lordy, you sure gave me a start! You want a room?"

"No, Thérèse, I want some information. I'd like to see the hotel guest register."

Thérèse Roger handed him a black book, worn out by frequent use and adultery.

"Monday, Tuesday, Wednesday. Ah, here we are! I would have staked my life on it. J.A. Bussières was here last night."

"Poor Monsieur Bussières. I heard what happened to him. So sad. He'd done so much for our region."

"Was he alone?"

"Monsieur Bussières? Yes, yes, yes."

Chief Dubuc planted his elbows on the counter and his two eyes into those of the owner.

"Thérèse Roger, I know you well enough to know when you've taken me for a big fool. Answer me honestly, now. Was J.A. really alone last night?"

"Actually no."

"So who was he with?"

She hesitated.

"Well, with a lady."

"With his wife?"

Thérèse Roger gave a Mona Lisa smile that said a lot.

"Yep, I would have eaten my moustache if I was wrong," concluded the police officer. "How old was she?"

"Oh, she was a young lady, I'd say about sixteen or seventeen, no more. But I only saw her on the sly, you know, because Monsieur Bussières sent her straight up to the room as soon as they got here."

"Did you know her?"

She shook her head.

"What time did they arrive?"

"Let's see. It was a bit after suppertime. Maybe eight o'clock. Monsieur Bussières checked in and went right up to unit eighteen, asking us to bring him champagne and pizza. He said he didn't want to be disturbed, you see, because the young lady was going to be interviewed for a job at his company."

Thérèse Roger leaned towards Chief Dubuc with a suggestive look and pursed her lips.

"Not that I believed that story. It's what he said every time anyway."

"J.A. came here often?"

"Most every Wednesday, and with a different young lady every time."

"Did he sign the registry every time?"

"Always. If you want my opinion, Monsieur Bussières lived the life he wanted, with whoever he wanted, and he didn't give a blessed nickel what other folks in Chesterville might think. Of course, he had the means to tell whoever he pleased to go to hell."

"That's my impression too. Give me the key to number eighteen."

Thérèse Roger handed it to him, apologetically.

"My housekeeper is sick and didn't clean up this morning. If you would rather wait until tomorrow, it will be cleaner."

Chief Dubuc was thrilled.

"No, no!" he cried. "Don't touch a thing!"

The chief of police and his deputy passed a series of motel units in a less than inviting state, strung along a grassy pathway sprinkled with pink flamingoes, before they got to number eighteen. Dubuc jiggled the key in the door. Leftover pizza and alcohol greeted them in the disorder of the room.

"Oh, my. There's been some hanky-panky here! Look at this, Lucien. Only the bed is still standing. Let's see if they've left any souvenirs."

The two men inspected the room with a fine-tooth comb for nearly half an hour, without uncovering anything of note. Lucien, who was starting in on the bed, suddenly turned to his boss.

"Come see this."

He lifted up the covers and showed him a red bloodstain in the middle of the sheet.

"You see," sighed Chief Dubuc, finally. "That confirms his good reputation."

Chapter 2

Leaning over the covers, Roméo Dubuc abruptly turned to his deputy, his nostrils flared.

"It smells like women's perfume. It comes from the pillow."

"Probably the girl who came up with Bussières. But let's check it out anyway."

Dubuc picked up the telephone and called the front desk. Thérèse Roger appeared in the entryway a few moments later, and caught the two police officers by surprise as they were noisily sniffing the pillow, like two hunting dogs sent out on a chase after a fresh scent. She leaned over herself.

"It's 'Interdit' by Givenchy," she said, without hesitating. I'd recognize that fragrance from a million others. It's the one my mother wears."

"Who in Chesterville wears that perfume?"

The hotel manager shrugged her shoulders.

"Oh, goodness, I couldn't say for sure. Ask Estelle. She works at Oasis Perfumes."

They got to the perfume store in the middle of the afternoon. Estelle Plamondon confirmed that she did carry Givenchy's 'Interdit' and had it in stock.

"Is it popular?"

"Fairly. 'Interdit' is a romantic and mysterious perfume from the 1950s, inspired by the actress Audrey Hepburn. I must have a dozen regular customers in Chesterville who buy it."

"I'm looking for names."

"Is it important?"

"Very."

Estelle Plamondon searched her memory.

"My best customer is a widow, Madame Latulippe. She's from . . . "

The policeman interrupted her.

"Madame Latulippe has one foot in the grave already. I'm looking for a young girl."

"How old?"

"Oh, I don't know, under twenty."

The woman shook her head. "Sorry. All my customers are at least forty. They grew up with 'Interdit.' You understand."

"Would you mind giving me their names? Who knows, maybe they have daughters who wear that perfume too."

*

Returning from the police station, Chief Dubuc prepared some strong coffee. A moment later, J.A. Bussières's chauffeur, Roland Fafard, came in to announce that Marguerita Bussières was now ready to talk to the police. He pronounced 'Marrrguerrrita' with a Spanish accent which made Chief Dubuc's ears buzz. Lucien hurried about, making room for two chairs in the Chief's office.

"I hope you'll excuse my mood at the cemetery this morning," whimpered the widow as she came in. "I'm just not myself since J.A. died. I still can't believe it's true."

"I understand," Chief Dubuc answered, motioning to her to sit down. "I have a question or two that I would like to ask you, if you don't mind."

"I'll try my best to be of use to you," she said with a forced smile.

She reached into her handbag to find something to wipe her eyes.

"Did you know if your husband was planning to go to the cemetery last night?"

"No, I spent the day in Sherbrooke yesterday, at my sister's, like I often do on Wednesday," she said, sniffling frequently. "I got back at nine o'clock, completely worn out. So I took a nice hot bath and I went to bed. I didn't wait up for J.A. In the evenings, he's often at the factory or at a meeting, and he's hard to get ahold of."

"So he had no real reason to go to the cemetery?"

"Listen, the only thing I could think of is that it was the twenty-fifth anniversary of his mother's death at the beginning of the week. It's possible that J.A. remembered at the last minute, went and grabbed a little bouquet of flowers and rushed off to the cemetery, even if it was eleven o'clock at night. If you knew my husband, Chief Dubuc, you'd know that he was quite capable of doing such a thing."

"In the pouring rain? J.A. must have really loved his mommy," Dubuc said, looking sceptical.

"You're right about that. J.A.'s mother helped make him the man he was. She left him a large piece of her fortune. When I met my husband sixteen years ago, Chief Dubuc, he wasn't going anywhere in life. But with his mother's inheritance, he bought himself a little duplex, and then another, and another one after that. Today the GalvaTech factory and J.A. Bussières Enterprises employ nearly 400 people in this area."

"I know all that, Madame. The whole village of Chesterville is still in shock over your husband's death, and I want to offer my sympathies. But I imagine that a man like him didn't only have friends in life."

"What do you mean?" exclaimed the widow, startled. She began to wiggle in her chair.

"Do you know anyone who disliked him enough to want to kill him?"

Marguerita Bussières suddenly came back to herself.

"I'm going to be very frank with you, Chief Dubuc. Several people detested my husband. I often heard about threats that people made, on the phone or in letters. But it was always anonymous, and J.A. didn't really take them seriously. I think he was pretty tough when it came to business. He had thick skin, in any case."

She fell into bitter and drawn-out sobs again. Her chauffeur wanted to take her outside, but Chief Dubuc gestured to him to leave her alone. He was determined to continue the conversation, even if it meant waiting patiently for a few moments, and signalled to Roland Fafard to leave the room. He did so, with half a heart or less.

Marguerita Bussières gradually composed herself.

"Lucien, bring me some strong coffee. Black. Would you be so kind?"

Chief Dubuc put on a rather phony air of cheerfulness.

"There, now, drink up. You'll be fit as a fiddle before you know it."

She smiled wanly.

The policeman got up and went over to sit down on the side of the desk, right in front of Marguerita Bussières. He seemed to be holding back a question that was burning his lips.

"I suppose you know that your husband had a few – how shall I put it – indiscretions?"

Amazingly, the widow pulled her head up high, pursed her lips and faced the question head on. Chief Dubuc noticed that the veins of her neck stuck out like violin strings and understood that he had hit the nail on the head.

"You're referring to his infidelity, I suppose? You bet I knew! The whole village of Chesterville was aware of it. I'm not stupid enough not to have noticed that my husband stepped out of an evening, Mr. Dubuc. J.A. cheated on me regularly and I knew it. Oh, at the beginning I did play the wounded wife. I cried. I broke things. But I figured out soon enough that chasing skirts was his second nature. When he saw a pretty face, it seemed to be too much for him to resist. Do you know what it's like, Chief Dubuc, for a woman to live, day and night, with the fear that her husband will leave her for someone else? Someone younger, prettier, sexier? That's how I lived for years. But, over time, we came to an agreement, J.A. and I. I agreed to close my eyes and not ask for a divorce, as long as he let me live my life as I pleased. As far as I was concerned, he could have as long a leash as he needed to play Don Juan. Anyway, we haven't – hadn't – had sexual relations for many years. In case you're interested."

"Well, no one would say you aren't up front about things. It mustn't have been much fun for you. Did you know any of his mistresses?"

"Not one. He didn't talk about them. That was part of our agreement. But I know that some of the girls were barely in their teens."

"Exactly," said Dubuc. "Lucien and I started our investigation, and it took us straight to the Motel Roger. According to our information, J.A. spent the evening with a young girl and . . . "

"It's quite possible," replied the widow dryly.

"Good Lord, is that all the effect it has on you?"

"What do you want me to do? Weep like a Madonna? Scream like a madwoman? I told you once, and I'll tell you again. I've come to terms with it. I've finally got to the point where I know what he's like. On the other hand, he *is* my husband. Was. And his death is horrible."

On that note, she got up, opened her Moroccan leather handbag and took out her cheque-book.

"Here is a cheque for $10,000," she said, poking the paper under the police officer's nose. "I hope that's enough to convince you of the importance of finding J.A.'s murderer."

Roméo Dubuc took the cheque, goggled with envy as he saw the amount written on it, and then gave it back to the widow with a heavy sigh.

"Give your money to charity, Madame," he said. "We've been told the Chesterville police force already gets paid way too much."

*

When Bussières's widow had left, Roméo Dubuc turned to his deputy.

"So what do you think?"

"About what?"

"About 'Marrrrguerrrita'? Cripes. I always heard that she was the dutiful and long-suffering wife. But I got shivers up my spine, listening to her. She's like the strong woman in the Gospels. Unless it's grief that's put her in that state."

"Did you see her eyes?" asked Lucien.

"It's hard not to notice a splotchy face like that! It looked like she learned how to do her makeup from the Cirque du Soleil!"

"Those eyes were full of fire," said Lucien. "When you were talking about J.A.'s affairs, her look was icy and her jaw was clenched like a boxer who was determined not to go down for the count. Let's both admit we were thinking she had some damn good reasons to rid the planet of J.A."

"Starting with vengeance!" Dubuc agreed.

"She was humiliated in plain sight of the whole town. And don't forget the inheritance. Bussières was worth a small fortune, from what I've heard tell of it. If Marguerita put up with his unfaithfulness for so many years, it was because she was set on keeping up her lifestyle. She was from a poor family. I imagine that J.A. made sure she'd have a golden retirement in Florida. At this point, Marguerita must feel like she's just won the grand prize in the 6/49."

"That's for sure," remarked Dubuc. "Money is always the principal motive in a murder case. Look for the heir and follow the scent: Marguerita, her son Conrad. Biron, the notary public, told me at lunchtime today that J.A. was leaving a fortune of almost four million dollars, divided equally between Marguerita and Conrad."

"It's Marguerita who's really going to gain from it," said Lucien, "because Conrad, J.A.'s son from a previous marriage, is in a mental hospital. It's a sad story."

While Lucien was lamenting the son's situation, Roméo Dubuc took out a huge ham and cheese sandwich from his drawer, unwrapped it and set it out in an appetizing display under his deputy's nose.

Lucien, who had been a strict vegetarian for several years now, couldn't help but take advantage of an opportunity to make his boss feel guilty. He teased him about his favourite indulgence.

"Oh, you can't be serious! A sandwich? At this time of day? Come on, you're just being a glutton."

The comment had the intended effect on Dubuc, who suddenly felt his stomach shrink. "I know, I know. But when you're built like a workhouse, the way I am, you have to eat that way too. You granola-suckers, you could go a week on a stock of celery. That's why you all look like walking skeletons. Look at you, Lucien. It's like you are standing behind an X-ray machine. You don't know what you're missing!"

Faced with his deputy's incredulous expression, he added in his own defence:

"If you really want to know, my dear fellow, I just finished a ten-day diet of reduced calories, sugar and fat."

"I didn't know you were on a diet."

"I had no choice," replied Dubuc with a resigned shrug. "Gilberte's got me up against a wall. 'Lose weight, you little piggy!,' she said."

"How many pounds did you lose?" asked Lucien, really interested now.

"Zero. Actually, I ended up gaining six pounds. But that's another story. The specialist explained to me that it's a natural phenomenon that often happens when you diet."

Lucien couldn't help but smile.

The phone rang.

"It's for you."

Dubuc's mouth was full. He shook his head.

"It's Moreau, the coroner."

Chief Dubuc jumped on the receiver, wiping his mouth on his shirt sleeve.

"Yes, Dr. Moreau. What? Very interesting. Go ahead." He scribbled down a few notes. "Oh, I see. Are you sure? Very well. Let me know what else you find out."

"Anything new?"

"Yes and no. Dr. Moreau did the first examination. He confirmed that the time of death was between eleven o'clock in the evening and one in the morning. The cause of death was two sharp blows to the chest, probably with a knife blade that penetrated the heart. The stabs wounds were clean. While we wait for the autopsy results, Dr. Moreau also informed us of some contusions on the shoulders, but nothing serious, just bruises, really."

"And the facial injuries?" asked Lucien.

"We have to wait for the autopsy to be finished for those. The doctor's going to call me back. As I expected, he also got a sample of fresh sperm, and you won't be surprised to hear that J.A. also had a high level of alcohol in his bloodstream. Cripes, Lucien, we absolutely have got to find the girl who was with our Casanova when he had his last hard on."

*

The next night, the body of Joseph Albert Bussières was laid out for viewing at the F.X. Marcoux Funeral Parlour. From seven p.m. on, it was as if the spectacle of the death of Chesterville's most important citizen had become the most sought-after prize in the county. Some people had known the deceased well; others were fascinated and frightened, at the same time, by the reputation that had grown up around the hard-edged businessman over the years. For their part, Chief Dubuc and Lucien had agreed to spend the evening there, hoping to accumulate clues, or at least bits and pieces of conversation that might be of interest.

Dubuc met his deputy at the door.

"Great way to spend a Friday evening, eh?"

Lucien seemed just as resigned to his fate.

"When you figure that three-quarters of the population of Chesterville are going to be filing by tonight and tomorrow, we might just have some luck."

The body was laid out for viewing in the biggest room in the funeral home. The casket had been closed, because of the horrible injuries to his face. The quiet room, measuring twenty metres by fifteen, was decorated with heavy burgundy drapes and was overwhelmed by fragrant bouquets and wreaths, to the point that the managers needed to place several of them in a second room. Chief Dubuc and his deputy had to elbow through the approximately 200 people present in order to make their way to the deceased. The Knights of Columbus were well represented, paying tribute to J.A., who was a Fourth Degree member. Chief Dubuc also noticed a dozen members of the Army of Mary who were noisily counting off their rosaries near the coffin.

"Poor J.A. I wonder if thousands of Hail Marys will save him a single minute of Hell."

Not far from the coffin, they noticed Bussières's widow, dressed in a long black dress and a veil that nearly completely covered her face. A few steps away from her, Chief Dubuc noticed Stanley Rubinsky standing discreetly off to one side. Dr. Rubinsky was the chief of staff at the Chesterville Psychiatric Hospital, the largest psychiatric facility in the region. But there was no sign of Conrad, J.A.'s son, who was a patient there.

Chief Dubuc shook the psychiatrist's hand and led him off to a corner of the room.

"J.A.'s death hasn't upset Conrad too much, I hope?"

"Gosh! The least you could say is that they weren't exactly the best of friends, you know," replied Stanley Rubinsky, with the New York Jewish accent that he still had after fifteen years of living in Québec. "Especially since it was his father who insisted on having him committed."

"Why do you suppose J.A. did that?"

"Well, hard to say. He thought that Conrad was very ill and that it was up to society to care for him. He felt he had done his share."

"Conrad detested him?"

Behind his thick and severe-looking glasses, the psychiatrist blinked quickly and scratched his salt-and-pepper beard before answering. It was a nervous tic that Chief Dubuc had often noticed in him, especially when he was thinking something over.

"Let's say he often had rather bizarre thoughts about

him. In therapy, I try to help Conrad resolve his inner conflicts with his father. It's a rather slow process that may take some years, because the subconscious image he has constructed . . . "

The policeman nodded his head, suppressing a yawn of boredom. He raised his eyes to the clock on the wall and suddenly realized how ridiculous the situation was. Here he was, listening to a psychiatrist babble about the subconscious of a schizophrenic, in the middle of a funeral parlour on a Friday night.

As soon as the opportunity finally presented itself, he started to politely excuse himself. Just then, Jerry Ménard appeared near the exit. A few months ago, Ménard had become the new owner of the Greluche Bar, a tavern that had acquired a rather dubious reputation, due to its habit of hiring minors.

Dubuc, who could see that the man was looking for a way to avoid him like a tax collector, cleared a path through the crowd over to Ménard. He took hold of his sleeve and smiled broadly at him.

"Well, if it isn't our man Jerry himself! How come you're back in Chesterville? Did you miss us too much?"

Ménard floundered around like an energetic salmon jumping at the end of a fishing rod.

"Spare me your stupid jokes. I've paid my frigging debts to society, and I'm leading a clean life."

The police officer would have recognized his nasal drawl out of a thousand tape recordings.

"Clean? That's not a word I've heard come out of your mouth very often, there, Jerry. You're more the dirty dealings type, aren't you?"

The other man, who had calmed down a bit, handed him a business card nervously. The police officer read:

*** LA GRELUCHE BAR ***
RELAX IN PLEASANT COMPANY
FULL SERVICE BAR / TABLE SERVICE
SECOND BEVERAGE FREE
FROM 5 P.M. TO 7 P.M.
MONDAY TO WEDNESDAY INCLUSIVE
GÉRARD ("JERRY") MÉNARD, PROPRIETOR

"That's right. I had heard you changed holes. You're at the Greluche now."

Ménard seemed insulted.

"Look, I've worked like a lackey trying to give that club back its good reputation, Chief Dubuc."

"Judging by your gold watch, I'd say business was pretty good."

As the officer looked at him incredulously, Ménard took on the intonation of a circuit preacher who had just gone into retirement.

"I may have made mistakes in my life, and you're as well aware of them as I am. But when I reached my fiftieth birthday, I made the choice to give all that up. I told myself, 'Jerry, it's over. The drinking, gambling, and womanizing.'"

He placed his right hand on his heart, to testify to the sincerity of his words. Dubuc laughed.

"The new Jerry Ménard, I guess! How very touching. I'm on the verge of tears."

The other man hadn't expected laughter, and tried to escape the scene. The police officer nailed him to the floor with a tight grasp on his wrist.

"I hate to leave this conversation, Chief, but I need some fresh air. I forgot my pills, and I'm allergic to flowers.

Dubuc took him off to one side and asked him, in as serious a tone as he could manage: "What exactly are you doing here tonight?"

"Nothing special," retorted Ménard, still sniffling.

"Monsieur Bussières helped me out a few times, just like he did a lot of other people here."

"Were you business partners?"

"No way! Bussières wasn't my type."

"What do you mean?"

"He wanted to control everything, from what I've heard."

"Where were you last Wednesday night?"

"At the Greluche, like every other night."

"Do you have witnesses who can corroborate?"

Jerry Ménard smiled, showing yellowed and rotting teeth.

"Frig! Don't you trust me?"

"Not a bit. Do you have witnesses?"

"A ton of them. You want names?"

"I'll talk to you again later."

He let the man loose. Then, catching a whiff of Ménard's cheap aftershave, asked: "I believe your story about as much the claims of a tooth-pulling potion-vendor."

Ménard, reaching the end of his rope of patience, thumbed his nose at him as he scanned the room.

"Sophie! Come on, Girl, we're leaving."

No answer.

"Sophie!"

He pushed people aside as he made his way across the room, raising his voice.

The two police officers followed him. Jerry Ménard returned to the room where the corpse was exposed for viewing.

"What does she look like, this Sophie?" asked Lucien.

"Blonde, about ten years old, pretty tall but rather skinny for her age. She stuck to him like a grease-stain. Jerry had that kid with a girl who did striptease. The mom took off as soon as she popped."

Suddenly, a scream of terror froze their blood. A woman had just fainted at the sight of Sophie Ménard, who had climbed onto the closed casket of J.A. Bussières and straddled it like a rodeo horse, letting out shrieks of joy.

Chief Dubuc was the first to get to her, while the other visitors in the room stood paralyzed. He grabbed her shoulder firmly to pull her down, but the girl refused to budge, clinging desperately to the handles of the coffin while she screamed repeatedly. It took Ménard and Lucien's help to make her give in, but not before she struck out with her fists and feet flying in all directions.

"What in the world got into you, Sophie?" the police officer shouted, beside himself.

"I wanted to play with the man in the box."

Dubuc was flabbergasted.

"But it's a corpse, Sophie. The man is *dead*, for pity's sake."

Chapter 3

The next morning, Roméo Dubuc pulled himself out of bed with some difficulty. He hadn't slept a wink all night.

"This case is going to drive me nuts!" he grumbled to his wife, Gilberte, over breakfast. "It's giving me nightmares. Imagine! Now Bussières's widow wants to sue Jerry Ménard because his little Sophie climbed on J.A.'s casket."

"She's only a child," Gilberte remarked. "Nobody should fault her for it."

She had pronounced the words calmly, despite the fact that the situation inspired a strong sense of shame in her. She was a discreet woman, with both feet on the ground, and a former schoolteacher who had always been supportive of Roméo, getting him through the two major crises that had threatened their married life: her husband's alcoholism and the tragic death of their son only two years before.

The telephone rang. It was Estelle Plamodon, the owner of the perfume store.

"Have you found the young girl you were looking for?" she asked.

Dubuc answered that he hadn't.

"When you came in, Thursday afternoon, I didn't think of it right away. It occurred to me later. There *is* a young girl who buys 'Interdit' by Givenchy from me. She's been coming in for the last six months or so. She can't be more than eighteen."

"I hope you haven't mentioned it to anybody. It's a rather delicate situation," the police officer responded.

She assured him of her complete cooperation.

"My customer's name is Pauline Talbot."

"Talbot."

"Her father is Jules, the grocer. She came in and bought some about a month ago."

Roméo Dubuc leapt to his feet and turned to Gilberte.

"I know it's a Saturday morning, that I have to fix the fence, go to the garage and everything else. But I have to find that girl too, and there's no time to waste."

He looked at his wife with a regretful expression and went out. The policeman knew Jules and Lorraine Talbot well. They had three children. The oldest studied at the Université de Sherbrooke. The other was a mechanic; and Pauline, the youngest, had quit school and gone to work at the Kesner Hosiery Mills. He headed straight for the factory.

He opened the door of the main entrance and climbed the rusty iron stairs that led to the second floor of the Kesner Hosiery Mills. From up here, he had a perfect view of the ground floor, where twenty employees were busy at sewing machines upon which huge bobbins of multi-coloured threads were mounted, causing a deafening racket. The foreman came over to meet him.

"You're looking for somebody?" he asked in a loud voice.

"Pauline Talbot."

"Nothing serious, I hope?"

Dubuc shook his head.

The foreman beckoned to him to follow. They went down a level, wove in and out among the noisy sewing machines and finally came to the back of the large room. A young girl, barely out of her teens, leaning over a piece of material, shyly raised her eyes when they arrived.

"Chief Dubuc wants a word with you, Pauline," said the foreman.

They went into the employees' lounge, which was empty at this time of day. The foreman excused himself.

The young girl sat down nervously on one of the chairs placed along the window. From where she was sitting, the rays of late-June sun came in through the dusty windows and tenderly touched her face. Chief Dubuc could tell that she would have paid dearly to be able to be anywhere but here. She was wearing a simple T-shirt and jeans, but he had to admit that the little girl he had once known was now a grown woman. Her delicate hands were decorated with gold rings on each finger, and her red nails testified to Pauline's attention to her appearance. She was of medium build, shapely, and long chestnut hair flowed around her girlish face. He could certainly see how a vulture like Bussières could be attracted to her, thought the officer as he walked over to the vending machine for a drink.

"You want a soda pop, Pauline?"

She shook her head.

"I didn't do anything wrong."

He stood there without answering for a moment, leaning up against the vending machine.

"Fffff . . . I always have a beast of a time opening these darned cans. My wife says my hands are too big. Real seal's fins, she says. It's like these cans were made for six-year-olds to open."

"Does my dad know you're here?" she asked, in a halting voice.

"Jules? No, don't worry. Anyway, it's been a while since I've seen your father. Is he doing well?"

It was a technique Dubuc used frequently during questioning. He jumped all over the place instead of getting straight down to facts. It always seemed to get the witnesses off course.

"I'm in the middle on an investigation, and I'd like to know where you were last Wednesday night."

"Wednesday night? Why?"

"Just answer."

"At home."

"All evening?"

"Yeah, I think so."

"Are you sure?"

"Well, maybe not the whole evening."

"How about at eight o'clock?"

"I was at my friend Brigitte's house. We were listening to music. The Beatles."

"What if I told you I knew you were at the Motel Roger?"

The girl's face turned livid, convincing the police officer that he had hit the target. He continued: "At Motel Roger. With J.A. Bussières."

Pauline quickly lowered her head and started biting on her lips.

"If my father finds out, he'll kill me!"

"Jules doesn't like J.A., is that it?"

"He couldn't even stand the smell of him before."

"Before what?"

"Before."

Dubuc felt Pauline becoming unnerved. He only had to push her a tiny bit further.

"Before J.A. took your virginity, I'm guessing?"

Pauline stood up suddenly, extremely agitated.

"I didn't have anything to do with J.A.'s death. I wasn't even with him when it happened! He left the motel at about ten-thirty. I promised I'd be home before ten. I ran like an idiot all the way home, in the pouring rain, and I went straight to bed. I only found out about J.A.'s death the next morning, at the same time as everyone else in the village!"

Pauline Talbot kept her head down and her loud sniffles broke up her speech.

"It's like everyone hated J.A. Not me. He bought me everything my father could never afford to give me: a beautiful new watch, a gold chain, pretty clothes. He was good to me. Wednesday night was the first time I slept with him."

"An empty bottle of booze was found. Did the two of you get drunk at the motel?"

"Not me. I was too scared my dad would find out. But J.A. was drinking all night. Drunk, most of it."

"Even when he left?"

"Oh, yeah! It was about time he got out of there. He was starting to get ugly."

"Did he hit you?"

"No."

"Do you know where he went after he left?"

"Home. He probably took a short cut through the cemetery so he wouldn't attract any attention. J.A. hated cemeteries! And to think that's where he ended up being killed."

"It seems to me like you're awfully afraid of your father. Did Jules know about your affair with Bussières?"

"He caught us last week. It was a pretty bad scene. Horrible. Poor Daddy, he's a real mother hen with me. I get yelled at every time I come home late. It's gotten pretty tiresome. It's like he's forgotten I'm sixteen!"

Chief Dubuc let Pauline get back to her work and left the mill. He was preparing for his meeting with the girl's father. Jules Talbot had been a sergeant in the Canadian Armed Forces, but had to take early retirement because an errant bullet had injured him. He had a limp. With his pension money, he had bought a little grocery store in Chesterville. From the time he had spent in the army, he had retained an intransigent sense of order and an iron discipline that he applied to everything he did, in business and in family life.

The grocery story was in the centre of the village, right near the parish church. Chief Dubuc parked his car, pushed the door open and heard the familiar tinkling of the little bell. He was greeted by a smell of fresh meat that made his mouth water. The store seemed dim and dusty to him. He felt a warm breath on his back.

"You looking for me, Roméo?"

The policeman turned around. Jules Talbot was standing behind him, holding two cases of cans in his hands. The police officer noticed the veins sticking out of his muscular arms.

"I need to have a word with you, Jules."

"Come back into the office then. Lorraine is out for lunch. We'll be able to have a private conversation."

Talbot deposited the boxes and moved ahead with a clopping noise. He motioned to the policeman to follow him. They went to the very back of the grocery story, passed behind the meat counter and went into a small room where the air was close and the main attraction was a calendar of half-naked women.

The grocer slouched into a chair and gestured to Dubuc to sit down as well. He picked up a nail file from the desk and began to file his broad, square nails.

"I thought I'd see you at the funeral parlour last night," the policeman said, dropping the words casually.

"I'd rather die than see J.A.'s damned face."

"I understand you weren't the best friends in the world."

The other man slammed the file down on the desk and crossed his arms, trying to get control of his emotions.

"Listen, Roméo, if you're here to grill me about J.A. Bussières, you can damn well . . . "

"Come, now, don't get upset! You know as well as I do that Bussières was murdered and mutilated. I started my investigation, and it took me directly to your daughter."

The grocer replied by hammering his fist down on the desk in rage.

"You leave my Pauline out of this, get it? Leave her alone! My daughter has nothing to do with that bastard."

"Whatever you say, Jules. Actually, it's you I'm interested in."

The grocer looked at him, stupefied.

"Pauline told me you went crazy when you found out she was seeing Bussières. That wasn't long before his death. Admit it, you've got a heck of a good reason to get rid of him."

"I'm about to start frothing at the mouth, just thinking about it. True enough! Lorraine and I tried to give our children everything, but that included principles. Pauline is young, and quite impressionable. She was daydreaming of Prince Charming. And of course she liked to be spoiled. Bussières knew it and used that to get his hands on her. It was too much for Pauline. He drew her to him like a magnet. Like a magnet, I'm telling you!"

"Did your wife know?"

"Lorraine hid the truth from me for a month. But you know how rumours travel in this village. I was like the husband being cheated on who's the last to know."

"Someone had to put an end to it, is that it?"

"For sure, but not by killing Bussières. Even if I dreamed about it at night. I confess, Roméo, I would have gladly wrung that pig's neck. Do you know what he did with girls like my Pauline? Do you have any idea, Roméo? When one of my customers found out that Bussières was going after her, she told me what happened to her own daughter. Can you top this? He paid them to let him get them pregnant! Bussières has nothing more than a moron he's disowned and I heard he was prepared to do anything to get himself another heir. So he slept with the young girls in the area.

He would find a teenager, would deflower her, impregnate her and then give her a big cheque, promising her that he would take care of the baby's future. Bingo! Apparently most of the girls panicked at the last minute and had abortions. Imagine, Roméo, at sixteen or seventeen! That's what would have probably happened to my Pauline!"

The police officer contented himself with one question: "When did you last see Bussières?"

"I don't know. Three weeks ago, maybe."

"And Wednesday night, where were you?"

"Are you trying to insinuate that . . . "

"I'm not insinuating anything. Where were you?"

Jules Talbot got up abruptly.

"At the grocery store, like every Wednesday night. It's the day the produce comes in. I have to stock the shelves and displays for Thursday. Seventy-two cases to empty, that's enough to keep a man busy."

"Was Lorraine with you?"

"She always helps me Wednesday night. We got finished around midnight."

The police officer listened to his answer, chewing on the end of his pen, and then put his notebook back into his pocket.

"I'll be in touch, Jules."

Roméo Dubuc stood up and put out his hand. The other man did the same, obviously half-hearted about it. The policeman noticed several flesh wounds on his right wrist.

"Did you cut your hand?"

"Pauline's cat scratched me. It's a little demon."

*

When Roméo Dubuc left the grocery store, the old copper clock on the counter indicated that it was twelve-thirty. He was in a hurry because he had promised Gilberte he'd be back at around noon. The main street of Chesterville was deserted. As he went by City Hall, the police officer was surprised to see a white Jeep, impeccably clean, parked in front of the building. It had American license plates.

He pushed open the front door, which led into the basement, and ran straight into a tall redhead. She was sitting in the narrow staircase.

"I'm looking for the chief of police," she said.

"That's me. Roméo Dubuc. Have you been waiting long?"

"Not too long."

"Sorry. The police station is officially closed on the weekends during the summer, but my deputy or I are still on call at all times. May I help you?"

They went into the policeman's office. Dubuc noticed that his visitor was casting sidelong glances around the room.

"I've been here before. It was about fifteen years ago," she said. "I had stolen some apples; the farmer caught me and brought me here. It gave me such a scare I can still feel the shivers."

"Is that American jeep yours?"

She moved towards him and shook his hand.

"My name is Catherine Gagnon. I'm J.A. Bussières's niece. I came to Chesterville several times when I was little. In the summer. My mother died when I was very young and Uncle J.A. used to invite me to spend a few weeks with Conrad, to chase away my boredom. For the last five years, I've been living in Burlington, Vermont, with my daughter."

"I imagine it's your uncle's death that has brought you to Chesterville?"

"I came as quickly as possible after Aunt Marguerita called me on Thursday. She was really beside herself, the poor woman. I know that he had quite a reputation, but she stood by him all these years."

"How is she doing?"

"She's not at her best, as you can imagine. I surprised her twice yesterday, hiding out in the bathroom to cry. All of these people coming to visit and phoning her are trying to help, but I think she'd prefer to be alone."

Roméo Dubuc got up and went over to the basement window that overlooked the yard. A gentle breeze crossed the room.

"I knew your uncle well, Catherine. You don't mind if I call you by your first name? I didn't approve of his lifestyle, but he was beyond compare as a businessman. He did a lot for the economy of Chesterville. To be frank, I feel that I owe him something. When I first got here, twelve years ago, I was getting over a depression. I had been working in Montréal doing police investigations for fifteen years, and I had reached the end of my rope, you might say. A big burn-out. My wife Gilberte insisted that we move out to the country. She thought a change of pace would do us good. When I got here, I worked for a few months as a carpenter, because no one wanted to hire me as a police officer. In those days, your Uncle J.A. may have only been a city councillor, but he was the real boss on the municipal council. He was the one who gave me my first break."

"It's terrible, what's happened. Do you have any leads?"

"Yes and no. I have to say that the investigation is going pretty slowly; that's normal for a village like Chesterville. With 5,000 residents, everyone keeps track of everybody else's business. I learned that the hard way when I came here, you can trust me on that. At first, I used to joke that half of the village worked at the psychiatric hospital and the other half were being treated there. With 230 beds, it's the biggest special care facility for a hundred miles around! Anyway, someone set my car on fire – in broad daylight! Like that: poof! No witnesses. Nothing."

"People lock elbows here, is that what you're saying?"

"That's one way of putting it. Rumours move more quickly than official information, and that's never good for investigations. To start with, there's that renegade Jeannot Lejeune who thinks he's some sort of big detective. Miserable son of a gun! He writes the worst kind of idiocies in his rag."

"He's a newspaper reporter?" asked Catherine.

"He's a first-class bull-shitter, that's what he is. Lejeune had a career as a vacuum cleaner salesman and insurance agent, before stumbling into the job of 'mopologist' at the *Clarion Express*. Six months later, he decided to try his luck as a reporter. That was the day my ulcer flared up."

Feeling his blood pressure flare up now, the policeman changed the subject.

"Will you be staying long?"

Catherine shrugged her shoulders.

"Probably a few more days. I was discussing that with Aunt Marguerita this morning. She'd like me to help her settle a few matters."

"J.A.'s will, I imagine?"

The tone of the question seemed to make the young woman uncomfortable.

"What do you mean?" she retorted.

"You probably already know that J.A. put you in his will. He's leaving you $50,000, I believe. A pretty sum, wouldn't you say? Did you know?"

The police officer watched as Catherine's cheeks turned flaming red. She lowered her head again.

"Yes, Aunt Marguerita told me after the funeral. But I didn't expect anything. You have to believe me. I'm going to try to be as helpful to my aunt as I can be. Afterwards, I'll go back to Vermont to get ready for classes next semester."

"Are you studying there?"

"No, I teach sociology of religion at the State University."

"You're interested in the Bible and in religion then?"

Catherine Gagnon smiled. Either Chief Dubuc was trying to get her to talk, or else he was really interested in her work. She decided to play along.

"Have you ever heard of Hare Krishna and Jehovah's Witnesses?"

The question suddenly hardened the expression on the policeman's face, which had been pleasant up to that point.

"Don't tell me that you're a Witness!"

"Not at all. But I'm interested in the influence that groups like the Jehovahs have on society."

"Oh, well. That's better. What I could tell you about the problems we have with religious groups in Chesterville. It's not surprising that they've become as rare as government spending in the region. We welcome vacationers, two months of the year, on the shores of Lac des Sables. It keeps the economy of the village going. Whether it's carpet-brush peddlers or church-peddlers that bother them, it's the same thing. Those guys pay for their holy peace. But I can tell I'm boring you with my sermons."

Catherine repressed a polite yawn.

"Actually, I came to report the disappearance of my cat. My six-year-old daughter can't stop crying over it."

"What kind of cat?"

"An orange and black one, named Coconut."

"Did he run away?"

"No idea. We stopped at a canteen on the 116 to have breakfast, at about ten o'clock, and when we got back to the car Coconut was gone. I think someone stole him."

"You can be reached at Marguerita's if I need you?"

"With all the visitors, I figured it would be better if I got off her hands and stayed at the Green Valley Campground."

"Listen, Catherine. Off the top of my head, I'd say it doesn't look good. I don't want to discourage you, but pets are being stolen all over the area. Especially cats."

Chapter 4

Roméo Dubuc stepped out of the church and breathed the fresh Sunday morning air deep into his lungs. A little group had already gathered, as usual, on the church square. He joined them with obvious delight. It seemed that Sunday Mass, especially during the summer, was an opportunity for the villagers of Chesterville to get together amongst themselves, far from the dozens of vacationers that invaded the shores of Lac des Sables, descending on their cottages or the nearby campgrounds. The police officer went off to join Gilberte, who was talking with a cluster of women. Juliette Beaupré, a widow, who was about sixty but very spry, came up to Chief Dubuc and rubbed a sensuous index finger under his chin. As usual, she was weighed down under trinkets and gaudy jewellery that clinked and shone with a false brilliance whenever she made the slightest movement.

"Say, Roméo, you really ought to do something about all those darned alley cats."

"Alley cats, Madame Beaupré? Why? Do the cats keep you awake at night?"

"I live near the cemetery so I can rest in peace, if you know what I mean. But last Wednesday night, I thought that I was hallucinating. The strays were meowing all night!"

Roméo Dubuc was literally blinded by the reflection from one of her fake gems, glowing like a spotlight in the morning sun. He tried to concentrate, however. If he was not mistaken, Madame Beaupré lived on the west side of the cemetery, just a few steps away from the spot J.A. Bussières's body had been found.

"Last Wednesday night, you say? That's interesting."

"The meowing started at eleven o'clock, right after the news on the TV ended. That's when I go to bed. Their concert continued into the wee hours of the morning. As you can imagine, I didn't sleep a wink all night."

"It was that bad, eh?"

"It was horrible! I went out to yell at them to get lost, but it was like talking to a wall."

"I'll look after it, Madam."

"I knew you would, Roméo."

She winked at him coquettishly before disappearing into the crowd gathered on the square.

Intrigued by the widow's comments, Roméo Dubuc left Gilberte's side and headed directly to the police station. He phoned the Coroner, Dr. Moreau.

"Sorry to bother you on a Sunday morning, Doctor, but I need your expertise. Someone who lives near the cemetery swears that she heard cats the night of the murder. Is it possible that cats might have disfigured J.A., in your opinion?"

"Cats, you say?" exclaimed the coroner, surprised. "If you had said raccoons that were starving or rabid, well, that I could understand, no problem. But cats! Listen, Roméo, those are probably pets that belong to your neighbours or mine. They're well fed and healthy. They can huddle together at night to meow at the moon or mate, but what in the world would push a cat to disfigure a human being, would you say?"

"I don't know. Animals are sometimes like people. In a group, they might do things they wouldn't do alone."

"Possibly. But suppose some cats had decided to have some fun disfiguring the body of J.A. Bussières. Wouldn't they have bit him? That's typical of animal aggression. But I didn't find any bite-marks on the corpse, Roméo. None."

The policeman hung up, down in the dumps about the

turn his investigation had taken. While he was tearing out his hair, Lucien came out of his office.

"I was passing by and saw your car."

The other man couldn't help but smile. It was his deputy's way of showing he cared. His bachelor apartment, a few steps away from the office, gave him a chance to watch the comings and goings at the police station very closely. Even when he was off, he never hesitated to appear whenever he thought he could make himself useful.

"Still on the Bussières case, I bet. A fine and sunny Sunday morning!"

"Yeah, Beaupré's widow was complaining about cats keeping her up the whole night of the murder with their meowing. But the coroner doesn't think J.A. could have been disfigured by an animal."

"By his murderer then?"

"Maybe. But I just can't get my head around that possibility. Cripes, Lucien, who could hate Joseph Albert Bussières so much that they would rip off half his face?"

"Have you questioned Talbot?"

"Jules really wanted to dispose of Bussières. It was eating at him all the way down to his big toe. Apparently J.A. intended to get his girl pregnant. You know Jules the way I do, a former soldier who's continued to be impulsive and violent. He couldn't stand the idea that J.A. was interested in his little Pauline. While I was talking to him, I thought he was going to boil over like an overheated pot. I have no intention of leaving him an inch of his shoe sole to walk on. He claims that he spent Wednesday night with his wife, looking after the shipment of fruits and vegetables at the grocery store. As an alibi, it leaves a bit to be desired, I'd say."

★

The next day, at around nine-thirty in the morning, Chief Dubuc was surprised to see Catherine Gagnon reappear in the doorway of his office.

"Well, if it isn't J.A.'s niece! Have you found your kitty yet?"

"Not yet," she sighed. "We spent all afternoon yesterday searching around the canteen. But I'm about out of ideas, and my daughter, Marie-Ève, hasn't stopped crying."

"You don't have anybody to help you?" risked the police officer.

"You mean like a husband, a boyfriend, or a lover?" asked Catherine, wise to his scheme. "I've been divorced for two years and I'm as chaste as Mother Teresa ever since, if you really want to write a report on it."

Seeing the embarrassed look on the policeman's face, she burst out laughing.

"To be honest, my work at the university and my six-year-old daughter take up all my energy. I don't really have time to . . . "

She interrupted her thought. "I don't know why I keep telling you my life story. But I never thought an ordinary cat could become so important in my daughter's life."

"She's just a child. All you have to do is buy her another one."

"That's easier said than done. Her father and I bought Coconut before she was born. They've grown up together. He's her best friend."

"Okay, okay, I get it. Forget what I said. I don't mean to make light of things. It's just that I've been hearing about nothing but cats for three days straight. I'm starting to see them in my soup! How about going to have a look at the cemetery?"

She was startled.

"What a sinister thought!"

"No, no," replied Dubuc. "Your Coconut is probably alive and kicking his four legs. Apparently cats have been roaming around the cemetery at night. Go and check if he's around. You never know."

She shrugged her shoulders.

"At this point, I guess I have nothing to lose."

★

Catherine walked slowly up to the cemetery. Sheltered by century-old oak trees and majestic weeping willows, the spot could have been a peaceful haven, if it weren't for the fact that such tragic events had taken place there a few days before. The sound of a lawn mower attracted her attention. The cemetery superintendent, Antonio Grimaldi, approached the grilled gate with a less than welcoming look.

"It's closed until two o'clock on Mondays. Come back later."

"I've lost my cat, and the police chief suggested I come and have a look around the cemetery," she said with a tired expression.

Without removing his pout, Antonio Grimaldi opened the door for her, half-heartedly.

Catherine reassured him, saying she'd only stay for a few minutes. She came back shortly afterwards.

"I've checked everywhere and at least I know he isn't here. Are you the caretaker? I imagine you're the one who discovered the body of my uncle, J.A. Bussières."

Knitting his brow, the man looked at her even more suspiciously.

"He was your uncle?"

"J.A. was my godfather. I spent several summers in

Chesterville during my childhood. Do you mind if I ask you to show me the exact spot you found him?"

Antonio Grimaldi really did not want to. But the pretty woman standing in front of him, barely thirty years old, melted his hesitation like snow in sunlight. He shook his head with a resigned air and led his visitor to the scene of the crime. All around them, the midday heat seemed to give the place and the things they saw a vaporous, almost unreal dimension.

"Your uncle wasn't an angel," commented Grimaldi, his voice contorted with hesitation. "But I guess you knew that already."

Catherine walked away, unwilling to pursue the thread of the conversation. She crouched down beside the spot where the corpse had been found. The man watched her.

"Did you lose something?" he asked, as he moved away.

"I'm looking for some kind of a clue, anything that could help me find out something about my uncle's murder."

"Wait. I might have something for you."

He walked into the shed and came back with an object he handed to Catherine.

"I found this in the grass the day after the murder. It was about thirty feet away from the body."

It was an amulet showing a small black cat, hardly bigger than a coin, hanging on a tiny gold chain.

"You didn't give it to Chief Dubuc?"

The man grimaced.

"What for? Nothing proved that object had anything to do with the murder. Who says it wasn't lying in the grass for days? Ever since the company cutbacks, I only mow the lawn once a week. Keep it, if you're interested."

"Did you notice anything else?"

"Details aren't exactly my strong point. I already told the police that."

Catherine thanked him and walked off towards the exit. On her watch, she saw it was almost noon. Her stomach was in her feet, but the little discovery intrigued her. She took out the amulet and turned it around in all directions in the palm of her hand. Then she returned to the police station.

*

As Catherine was coming in, she was almost hit by a tornado that almost knocked her to the ground before sweeping her into the basement. A moment later, a shout echoed for two leagues around.

"Lejeune, get the hell out of here!"

Roméo Dubuc dropped his utensils noisily. He tore off the serviette that was hanging from his neck, while his spaghetti got cold under his eyes.

He stood up, walked over to the reporter who was still out of breath, and grabbed him forcibly by the shoulder.

"Lejeune, today you are outdoing yourself! My patience has its limits and my lunch hour is sacred! S-A-C-R-E-D. Do you hear? Next time you come in here, act like you're in a mosque. Take off your shoes, lower your head, and close your mouth!"

Unimpressed by the tone and the corrosive words of the police officer, Jeannot Lejeune was able to think on his feet. He decided to leave, but as he tried to escape a sharp pain in his left shoulder called him back into line.

"Can we make a trade?" he asked suddenly, feigning a pitiful look.

"What kind of a trade?" Dubuc thundered back.

"You keep me alive and I'll give you some privileged information that will help your investigation."

The other man relaxed his grip and folded his arms in a defensive gesture.

"I'm listening. Just don't try to trap me, my little son of a biddy."

Lejeune looked at the police officer and leaned his head in Catherine's direction. She hadn't missed a second of the drama.

"Is it safe to talk?"

"Absolutely. In fact, I urge you to get started right away."

The *Clarion* reporter took out a notebook and leafed through it nervously without taking his eyes off Catherine for a second.

"This lady is J.A.'s niece," Dubuc said.

Reassured, Jeannot Lejeune checked his notes as he spoke.

"You owe me big time for this one. According to my super-confidential sources, J.A. Bussières was seen with a VIP client at the Patchouli Italian Restaurant in Sherbrooke two days before his death. Apparently this guy owned him 80,000 bucks, and was six months behind in his payments. J.A. was heard saying to him, 'If I don't have my money by Friday at the latest, I'm going to break your effing legs.'"

Jeannot seemed proud of himself. Satisfied, he put his notebook back into his pocket and looked around him. Dubuc hadn't budged any more than an ice sculpture.

"That's it? No reaction? Golly, Chief, turn on your headlights! That guy's probably our murderer. He owed J.A. 80 K. That's a damn good reason to kill someone and clear your debts. In New York, people shoot each other for thirty cents. You should know that if anyone does."

Roméo Dubuc returned to his spaghetti, heaving a sigh.

"You and your gull darn confidential information! The last time I trusted you, I ended up biting my nails for six months straight afterwards. Your information is about as reliable as tomorrow's weather forecast, my boy. Do you at least have an eye witness? The name of J.A.'s client? His phone number? Something tangible to help out with the investigation? For pity's sake!"

Lejeune took his notebook out again and flipped feverishly through the pages.

"All you had to do was ask!" grumbled the reporter. "I wrote down the name of the client. It's right here. Jean-Yves."

"Jean-Yves what?" asked Dubuc, suddenly taking an interest.

Lejeune raised his eyes to the ceiling in desperation.

"Look, I wrote it down somewhere."

"Jean-Yves what?" repeated Dubuc impatiently, tapping a rhythm out with his fingers on the table.

"Just Jean-Yves," Lejeune finally managed to spit out.

The police officer stood up, his impatience reaching its breaking point.

"How far do you think we'll get with just a first name, Lejeune? It's like turning a town upside down to try to find a dog named Fido!"

"Talk about ungrateful! Here I am, trying to help you, and you're asking me for the moon. I'm not the one leading the investigation."

"That's just it, my boy. That's exactly true. You go do your job and we'll do ours. Now, get the hell out of here!"

Offended, Lejeune cast a glance of disdain towards the police officer's plate of spaghetti as he headed out the door.

Catherine had remained silent, shyly standing with her back against the door. She was biting her lips at the sight of Roméo Dubuc's superhuman efforts to keep his composure. After an instant that seemed to last for centuries, he motioned to her to come over.

"Every time I see that guy I start dreaming of my retirement. That son of a half-cocked gun! But forgive me for acting like an ape in a uniform, Catherine. Lejeune plays on my nerves. There should be a law against letting ugly bugs like him write in a newspaper."

"He's following the investigation?"

"Anything that can make a good scandal, that's what Lejeune's after. He's drawn quite a few flames from a lot of people in Chesterville over the years. He twists the truth so he can write these stories that make no more sense than a soap opera. Last time he dropped one of his famous "leads," as he calls them, on my lap, I surrounded an old hog house with twelve officers from the Sûreté du Québec at the Chesterville exit. According to the so-called "privileged information" Lejeune had, the owner was hiding a still in the basement of a pork farm. Well, Madam, guess what? We ended up turning the place upside down and there wasn't a drop of alcohol anywhere. Not a single drop! But we smelled like pigs for two weeks afterwards. The guys from the Sûreté probably still hate me for it. Anyway, enough about Lejeune. I imagine you're back from the cemetery."

"Yes, and you were right. I found the cat."

"You see? I told you."

"But not my cat."

Catherine reached into her pocket and took out the little amulet with the black cat on it, and dangled it from the gold chain, looking as if she was enjoying herself.

"The caretaker at the cemetery found it about thirty feet away from my uncle's body, a day after the murder. But it's possible it was just lying in the grass for a few days. It's pretty, don't you think?"

But Roméo Dubuc wasn't listening to her. His gaze was fixed on the charm that danced before his eyes. Catherine saw large drops of sweat pearling on the police officer's forehead. He swallowed his saliva with difficulty.

"Is something wrong?"

Without replying, Dubuc took Catherine into his office, closed the door noisily behind him and sat her down in a chair. He didn't say a word for a long time, standing with his hands clasped in front of him, before raising a pathetic look towards his visitor.

"Catherine, do you believe in the devil?"

Chapter 5

The question cracked like a whip through the humid air of the office. Roméo Dubuc was a solid chap who didn't seem easily flustered. But Catherine couldn't help but notice that the man sitting in front of her was completely distraught.

"Are you serious?"

"I've never been more serious in my life. You're a well-educated woman, a university prof. I bet you've tossed those questions around in your head. So tell me honestly, do you believe in the devil?"

Catherine paused for a long while to think it over.

"I'm not sure what to say. In the United States, two Americans out of three truly believe that the devil exists. Whether he's called Satan, Beelzebub, the god of the underworld, or simply the devil, he represents the forces of evil. Personally, I think that Satan symbolizes what is most evil in the inner life of a human being. In the name of Satan, certain people will carry out repulsive acts that they would never do otherwise. In the Middle Ages, people believed that spirits . . . "

The policeman interrupted her with a gesture of impatience.

"Enough of the sociology lectures, please. Just tell me whether it's possible for intelligent people to worship the devil."

"Are you talking about satanism?"

Dubuc's only response was to stand up, open a cupboard and take out a thick file that he deposited under the young woman's nose.

"This is the Chainey case. A file that's as thick as the

New York City phonebook. I swear to you, that affair turned everybody inside out in Chesterville."

As Catherine stared, wide-eyed and speechless, he continued.

"The case is two years old. Imagine this: a young student, nineteen years old, named André Chainey. A good guy, the pride and joy of his family. And hard-working too. He worked as a stock boy at Talbot's grocery store on the weekends. André was finishing Cégep and was supposed to go into Business Administration at the Université de Sherbrooke the next year. He was tops in his class, a real genius. You know the type. Well, that's where it starts getting complicated. Not long before the end of the school year, André underwent a personality change, practically overnight. He quit his job, stopped going to class, went on drinking binges, started hanging out with punks, smoked pot and I don't know what else. From what people said, he had fallen in love with a girl named Liette Bardois, of unknown address, a girl who was pretty bizarre. To make a long story short, André went – let's see, it was May 7th, to a party organized in the abandoned Protestant church on the 8th line, less than a mile from Chesterville. At eleven thirty-four p.m., quite exactly, we got a call from a farmer nearby who was complaining that the kids were causing a ruckus. I went out there myself, and what I found there was a party, my dear lady. A real orgy! A gang of hooligans, heavy metal music playing full blast, dope, drink, the whole bit. And in the middle of all of it, a big bottle of pills for high blood pressure. The kids were gobbling them like Smarties! André Chainey died in the ambulance on the way to the hospital. Coroner Moreau listed the cause of death as an overdose of pills."

"Do you have any reason to doubt him?" asked Catherine.

"I said it once and I'll say it again: André Chainey was

a really brilliant guy. Far too intelligent to "accidentally" take too many pills."

"Do you think someone killed him?"

"Killed him? No. But I have reason to believe they pushed him to the point of suicide."

The police officer opened the drawer and handed Catherine a series of black and white photos, taken on the site of the tragedy. On the first photo, she recognized in the foreground the symbol of the antichrist, number 666, painted on one of the walls in the old church where the drama had taken place. Another photo showed a pentagram, a five-pointed star that had been drawn awkwardly with chalk on the floor.

"Those are well-known satanic symbols," she remarked. "But they don't really prove anything. Any little trickster can amuse himself scribbling on abandoned buildings."

Roméo Dubuc agreed.

"What you just explained to me in thirty seconds took me a year to figure out, with my limited means. During the investigation, the Sûreté du Québec admitted that there were satanic elements in the old church, but refused to see it as anything more than a young people's party gone bad. But was it just a rowdy party that night? Or was André Chainey a member of some satanic cult? I have no idea, and the poor boy took his secret with him to the grave."

The police man slouched into his chair and crossed his arms. Catherine felt he was totally distraught.

"This thing is still bugging you two years later?"

Roméo Dubuc fought back his tears.

"I guess I can tell you. André Chainey was my son, my adopted son. My wife Gilberte and I raised him like our own boy. His death was a terrible shock and I went through a long, dark period. The night of André's death, I found this in his pocket."

He opened his drawer and placed a small object in front of Catherine. It was an exact replica of the black cat pendant she had just brought back from the cemetery.

"Do you see why I'm worried? I don't mind letting the dead rest in peace. André's no longer with us and nothing can bring my son back to me. But what you discovered in the cemetery next to your uncle's corpse could have implications that are much more serious than I first imagined."

Catherine tried to follow his reasoning attentively.

"You mean this little pendant . . . "

The police officer's words seemed to be suspended in mid-air. "Go on."

" . . . Might be some kind of a . . . fetish object?"

"Continue."

Catherine weighed each word carefully.

" . . . Belonging to . . . "

Chief Dubuc showed his agreement, nodding his head vigorously.

" . . . Belonging to a strange organization?" Catherine concluded, looking rather sceptical.

He shrugged his shoulders and stood up.

"I don't know yet. But what I do know is that this fetish seems to attract death all around it."

*

After Catherine left, the policeman went over to find Lucien and told him about his concerns. More than ever, he needed to get some advice from his old comrade-in-arms. Lucien had seen, first hand, how the private drama that led up to André's death had unfolded, and knew how this tragedy had gradually sapped his boss's energies. Dubuc seemed to be searching for answers deep in the eyes of the mysterious black cat dangling from the little gold chain.

"What was it doing there on the grounds of the cemetery?"

Lucien listened as his boss recounted Catherine's discovery.

"I understand why you're so upset, but we have a corpse on our hands and a murderer on the loose. I might sound hard-hearted, but let's be realistic: we have to solve J.A. Bussières's murder.

Chief Dubuc wiped his damp eyes.

"You're right, Old Boy, I'm getting carried away with my memories of André. I've never been able to get closure on his death. It will keep me up nights for the rest of my life. I'll probably never know whether my boy was just scribbling satanic symbols on walls or if he was flirting with the devil."

"I'll tell you again, Chief," Lucien said calmly. "J.A. Bussières's death was a brutal murder; the victim was disfigured. We know that much. But until we prove otherwise, an old mistress or a jealous husband could have done the deed. You said so yourself. Anyway, as far as I know, we didn't find J.A. with his throat slit, or burned at the stake, or exorcised."

Roméo Dubuc agreed with a nod of his head. His deputy had spoken slowly, articulating each word. His common sense had worked miracles once more.

"As for Jules Talbot . . . " continued Lucien.

"Jules had the best motive in the world to kill J.A.," replied Dubuc. "He was roaming around Pauline like a fox beside a chicken coop, and Jules had already warned him to keep his distance."

The telephone rang.

"Police Station. Hello, Dr. Rubinsky. What? Whenever you'd like. In fifteen minutes? Perfect."

He hung up the receiver.

"Stan Rubinsky is on his way over. Apparently he has some interesting information about our investigation. Gee whiz, my spaghetti's going to end up in the garbage can again."

The chief psychiatrist from the Chesterville hospital came in a very minutes later.

"I'm sorry to disturb you by coming in with so little notice," he said, looking around for a chair. "I'm taking advantage of my lunch hour."

Roméo Dubuc looked at him rather resentfully.

"Me too, Doctor. I was trying . . . "

"Now you know why doctors get ulcers." the psychiatrist joked. "I've been lucky up until now. I often eat in the middle of the afternoon, or else in the early evening! It reminds me of when I was a doctor in Vietnam in the early 1970s. We sometimes went whole days without eating, there were so many wounded to keep us busy!"

He sat down, stroked his salt-and-pepper beard and examined Chief Dubuc a moment before he began to talk.

"I hesitated to come over and talk to you. You understand – it's rather confidential. I wanted to talk to you about Conrad."

"J.A.'s son?"

"About a week ago, he got the idea in his head that he'd refuse to take his medication. When the nurse gave him his pills, he'd take them, hide them under his tongue and then spit them out as soon as her back was turned. We called his father, who came to see him right away."

"I thought the two of them detested each other," said the police officer, surprised.

"That's true, but if you want my opinion, J.A. loved Conrad, deep down. From what I've been able to understand, it's Marguerita, J.A.'s second wife, who detested the child and managed to convince J.A. to put him in an institution. The outcome was that J.A. Bussières completely ignored his son, except in the case of an emergency. During his last visit, things took a bad turn."

"What do you mean?"

"Conrad began to show characteristic signs of a relapse into schizophrenia. That could be expected, given the fact he wasn't being medicated properly. During J.A.'s visit, an argument broke out. J.A. insulted him and Conrad, who was out of control, threw a chair over his head. His father left, slamming the door, and Conrad became withdrawn."

"And then?"

"Well, that's the reason for my visit," explained the psychiatrist. "I thought you'd want to know. Conrad escaped from the hospital the day his father died. The nurse on duty saw he was missing at about two o'clock in the afternoon."

"Escaped?"

"Gosh! He broke a window in the bathroom, jumped from the third floor and took off. A real James Bond!"

The policeman raged:

"And you're telling us this only now, Dr. Rubinsky?"

The other man tried to calm him down.

"Listen, I wanted to keep it a secret out of respect for Marguerita, that's all. With J.A.'s death, it really wasn't the time to inflict another trial on her, the poor woman. But enough time has passed, and the situation is making me concerned. That's why I sent out two orderlies to search for him. You know, it isn't the first time Conrad's taken French leave from us. But, in the past, he was satisfied with hanging around in the neighbourhood, which was reassuring. If we had to contact the police every time one of our patients got loose . . ."

Dubuc had to admit that was true.

"Yes, I must say – it's like your hospital is a sieve, Dr. Rubinsky!"

"Don't worry. Chesterville isn't Montréal. Sooner or later, hunger, the cold or the police always bring them back to us."

"He disappeared five days ago?"

"Five."

Dubuc turned to his deputy.

"Lucien, phone the Sûreté du Québec and report Conrad Bussières missing. Tell them to check in the next county too, in case he had the great idea of hitching a ride somewhere."

Stanley Rubinsky stood up.

"And tell them, as well, that he is getting more dangerous by the day. When Conrad isn't taking his medication . . . Good Lord! He's capable of anything!"

"Is Conrad violent with the other patients?"

"More so with the hospital staff. You know, he reacts very badly to any form of authority when his state of mind is not under control. Whether it's his father, the wardens or even his psychiatrist."

"What do you mean?" asked Lucien.

Dr. Rubinsky's only response was to stand up, unbutton the cuff of his well-pressed white shirt, roll up the sleeves and show the two police officers a horrible scar on his right forearm.

"Cripes! Did Conrad bite you?" said Dubuc, startled.

"It was two years ago. If you find him, be careful. Like I said, he can be like a rabid animal."

*

Catherine glanced at her watch. It was almost four o'clock in the afternoon. She stepped on the accelerator of the Jeep and took off down the road in a cloud of smoke. Since her divorce, she was constantly worrying about her daughter,

Marie-Ève. She had obtained custody after a hearing that had left her feeling quite bitter about her ex-husband as well as the justice system in general.

When she arrived, she hurried over to the tent. Nobody there. She had expected to find Marie-Ève and Barbara. Barbara Watkins was a sixteen-year-old teenager, the daughter of a neighbour in Burlington. She had been so insistent about coming to spend a few days in Québec that Catherine hadn't been able to refuse her. After all, she was a little like a big sister who took charge of Marie-Ève. But for the moment, neither one was around the area and Catherine was concerned.

The campground was overflowing with activity. It was a large strip of lush green sites located between Highway 116 and the Lac des Sables, where tents and campers lined up obediently. Catherine could make out a group of teenagers in bathing suits playing volleyball, not far from where she was standing, and close by the playground was full of children. But there was no trace of Marie-Ève and Barbara.

Catherine ventured to the outskirts of the grounds, where the freshly-cut grass suddenly gave way to weeds and bushes. She made her way slowly, pushing aside the branches that brushed against her face. Catherine took the risk of going down a narrow pathway, just wide enough to let a hiker pass between the trees. Above her head, greenery that became thicker as she walked blocked the sun. She stopped short when she heard footsteps. She detoured to the right, beating down a thick carpet of ferns and moss that led directly to the pond adjoining the Lac des Sables. Catherine grabbed hold of the trees to slow her awkward and slippery descent. She thought she heard children's voices close by.

"Marie-Ève! Barbara! Where are you?"

After an instant of silencc, a familiar voice called out:

"Here, Mama! Near the water! Come here faaaast!"

Her heart beating up a storm, Catherine raced down the last few metres separating her from the pond.

"I'm coming, Marie-Ève!"

Catherine reached the shores of the water. She could see Marie-Ève crouching on a large, flat rock, holding her cat, Coconut, in her arms. Barbara and another girl were keeping her company.

"You found Coconut, Darling! I'm so happy!"

She picked her up and hugged her. Then she stroked Barbara's curly crop of hair. Barbara could tell that Catherine was worried.

"It's my new friend who found Coconut," Marie-Ève said. "Look, he's all dirty. I'm going to give him a bath. Can you help me wash him?"

"Let's go to the tent, instead, Dear. Barbara and you can look after Coconut there."

"Can my friend come too?"

"Of course."

The four of them climbed the steep hill and headed back. Marie-Ève was beside herself with joy and told Coconut everything that had happened since he disappeared. Then she turned towards the little girl and put the cat in her arms.

"You can hold him too, Sophie, but only because you're my friend."

⋆

Jules Talbot was as enraged as a lion in a cage. Dubuc had summoned him to the Police Station and was still interrogating him more than an hour later. The grocer was even more irritated by the fact that the police officer seemed to be prepared to draw out the suffering as long as possible.

Talbot finished his third cup of coffee, while the policeman paced nervously around in the little interrogation room.

"Stop going around in circles, Roméo! You're making me dizzy!"

The policeman stopped short. "We'll go through this one more time, Jules. I want you to explain to me why . . . "

"Listen, here," the other man said, trying to control his impatience. "I would be happy to sign a confession in my very best handwriting, but I didn't kill that cockroach! So let's get this J.A. Bussières thing over with once and for all, because I need to do the store closing before supper time!"

Dubuc's only reply was to sit down in front of the grocer.

"I know you threatened J.A. in your grocery store. We have witnesses. You called him a 'goddamn bastard who didn't deserve to live.' I have two eye-witness testimonies. Are you going to try to deny that too?"

"It's very possible that my words went beyond my thinking. You know that I'm a little impulsive in any case. But if I had killed J.A., I wouldn't have stabbed him."

"You wouldn't?"

"No, Sir! If you want to know the whole truth, I would have let him bleed out, very slowly, by strangling him with chicken wire. I would have made the agony last for hours and hours. Now that you know my feelings about him, give me a break and go out and find the real murderer. My work is waiting for me."

The policeman let Talbot kick up his heels like rodeo horse until he ran out of breath. Then he asked him the same question yet again.

"Where were you at eleven o'clock last Wednesday?"

"For the hundredth time: I was in the warehouse unpacking the vegetables. I was getting ready for our big day on Thursday. If you don't believe me, ask Lorraine."

"Lorraine is your wife."

"She may be my wife, but she's not a liar! Didn't she tell you I was there?"

"She told me you were with her all evening."

"Okay, then. What more do you need?"

"Lorraine also told me that you were in the warehouse most of the night and she was in the store."

"What difference does that make?"

"All the difference in the world. You could have easily left the warehouse without anyone noticing," the police officer replied dryly.

Talbot spread his arms out on the table and lit a Player's. It was his fifth cigarette since arriving at the station.

"I didn't know you still smoked like a locomotive," the officer said.

"It's a horrible habit I've never managed to break."

"And yet you're a man of great willpower. You were in the army."

"That doesn't mean anything. Tons of guys in the army smoke."

"But they don't all swim under the ice in winter."

The grocer abruptly put his cigarette down and glared at Dubuc.

"Where exactly are you going with all this?"

"To the bet that you made with some guys to swim naked under the ice in the middle of January. Is that true?"

The other man laughed nervously.

"You did your research."

"So is it true or not?"

Talbot nodded that it was.

"It's ancient history. I was nineteen years old at the time and I was in Valcartier. The guys dared me to swim buck-naked under the ice on January 22nd, at twenty degrees below zero. I did it, and that's the end of the story. Nothing out of the ordinary."

"Maybe not, but the other recruit that did it with you was practically frozen to death. Why him and not you?"

"Dunno. Maybe my skin is tougher than the other guy's."

The grocer looked at his watch and fidgeted impatiently.

"If you're going to hold me up any longer, Roméo, you're going to have to put me in jail. It's almost four o'clock and Lorraine will have to close up by herself."

Jules Talbot stood up. His hard and unblinking stare plunged into that of Chief Dubuc. The policeman understood that there was no point trying to keep him from leaving.

"I can't hold you, Jules. At least, not yet."

Chapter 6

"I came to offer you a beer."

Catherine Gagnon was stupefied. Chief Dubuc arrived at her tent sponging his forehead; his shirt was marked by large spots under his arms. It was early evening, and the July heat was slowly settling down on the Green Valley campground.

"Offer me a beer?"

Catherine burst out laughing, turning the hamburgers over on the grill above the propane stove.

"After watching you soaking in sweat like that, I think I'm the one who should be giving you one. Do you want something to drink?"

"No alcohol. But I wouldn't turn down a glass of water. When it's as hot as it is today, I almost miss my snowblower.

He turned towards Marie-Ève and Barbara Watkins.

"Are these your daughters?"

"Only the younger one. Barbara is a friend of Marie-Ève. She's an American girl from Vermont who doesn't speak French. Can you get by in English, Chief Dubuc?"

The police officer grimaced.

"Like a Spanish cow!"

Nevertheless, he approached the girls and tried to get to know them as best he could. He took a wooden match, placed it in the palm of his hand, and then closed his fist, managing to get the girls' attention.

"Where is the match?"

Without hesitation, Marie-Ève pointed to the left hand. Barbara did the same. Dubuc opened his fist. Empty. The girls pointed to the right hand. He opened it. Also empty. He burst out laughing at the sight of the astonished faces of the girls, not to mention Catherine, who hadn't missed a beat.

"Are you a magician or what?"

Instead of answering, Dubuc asked Marie-Ève to lift up his cap. The match fell to the ground.

"It's magic!" cried out Marie-Ève, her eyes dropping to her sides in surprise. "Magic!"

Barbara Watkins was also under Medusa's spell, trying her best to put together her few words of French, unfortunately too late to express her surprise.

"I do a bit of prevention in the schools around here," explained Dubuc. "Children are a demanding audience. They like you or they don't. You need to have a lot up your sleeve. So at the beginning of my presentation I often capture their interest with this old trick. I have to say it works every time."

While he was talking, Catherine set the table.

"I don't really like arriving on someone's doorstep at mealtime," added the policeman, seeing that Catherine had set an extra place. "I came to ask you if you wanted to come with me to the Greluche Bar tonight. I want to make a courtesy visit to Jerry Ménard around nine o'clock, and I was thinking that with your expertise it would be good if you could have a look around, especially in Jerry's office. I'm looking for clues, anything that could give me more information about your uncle's death."

"Is Jerry a suspect?"

"Yes and no. He's a guy with a pretty shady record, a jail term for fraud, that kind of thing. At the time, he was hanging around with the worst vermin in the county. To tell you the truth, I wouldn't touch that guy with a thirty-foot pole! I saw him again at the funeral parlour. Jerry had disappeared from the area for a few years, and he only came back a few months ago, when he bought the Greluche. I want to know what he's doing around here."

Catherine agreed. They arranged to meet at the Police Station at nine o'clock.

★

Dubuc had parked his private car behind the station and traded his uniform in for more discreet clothes. He beckoned to Catherine to get into his car.

"My old Buick probably won't attract as much attention as the patrol car. I should probably have warned you that the Greluche is not a very reputable establishment."

"Are you worried about me?" Catherine asked, smiling.

He hesitated.

"It's not a reputable place. But I prefer going there at night, when the tavern is full. That's when you have the best chance of seeing and hearing interesting things."

They parked the Buick at the back of the gravel driveway and walked across the parking lot, weaving their way through the cars. Near the entrance, Catherine noticed three or four bikers talking noisily beside their bikes. One of them turned and whistled at Catherine as they walked by. She ignored him. On the neon sign above their heads flickered the silhouette of a seductive dancer, every ten seconds or so. It was obvious what the place was for.

"But this is a strip joint!" shouted Catherine.

The police officer tried to reassure her.

"I told you the Greluche wasn't exactly a convent. Do you still want to come in with me?"

Catherine wasn't really interested, but she felt it was too late to decline.

The Greluche was an old, abandoned warehouse that had been renovated. It was long and narrow, with round tables placed around a dance floor in the middle. Giant mirrors along the walls multiplied the reflections of the lights hanging over the dance floor. At the very back, the bar welcomed a continuous stream of waitresses coming and going between customers to get to the tables. The entrance to the room was guarded by a bouncer who looked like an early descendant of the Cro-Magnon man. He growled and reluctantly stepped aside to let the police officer and Catherine through.

The rhythm of disco music got the better of Catherine, who instinctively headed to the dance floor, her hips swinging. Dubuc headed off, telling her:

"You stay here. I'm going to go and have a look for Jerry."

The police officer went down the hallway behind the bar, passing three doors with signs reading "Management – Keep Out." He tried the knob on each one of them: locked. He stopped in front of the second one and checked around him. There was nobody in sight. Reassured, he kneed the door, near the doorknob, and it gave way. He went in.

The room was messy beyond imagining. It was going to be like looking for a needle in a haystack, Dubuc told himself. He turned on a lamp that gave out a feeble light. Dubuc got to work searching the dim room. He could feel china, empty cases of liquor, coats, electrical tools, a pitiful disorder that reminded him suddenly of the sad state of his own basement.

Suddenly, the police officer froze. He could hear murmurs. He posted himself behind the door and reached for his revolver, his eyes locked on the doorknob and his heart beating in his throat. The murmurs got louder. Dubuc turned around. The noise was coming from inside the room; he was sure of it. Still clasping his gun against his body, he moved towards a little cupboard that measured about one square metre which had been cut out of one of the walls of the office. The police officer stepped forward, his index finger on the trigger, and opened the door. A little girl was sitting on the floor, practically folded over on herself in the cramped obscurity. She was humming, unmoved by the fright she had caused him.

"Sophie! My God, what are you doing in here?"

He leaned over and helped her. She had trouble standing on her weak legs. Sophie Ménard had a dirty face and filthy hands. She rubbed her eyes constantly, still humming.

"How long have you been in there?"

"Not long."

She pointed to the number six on the clock on the desk.

"You've been here all evening? This place is about as big as the palm of my hand! You could have died in there."

"I do it a lot."

"Is your father punishing you for something?"

"No, but I like to be alone to talk to my friends."

"Oh, I see. And what are your friends' names?"

"There's Poppy the dinosaur, and Fatua, the horse with wings, and then there's . . . "

One thing was for sure, Dubuc thought. The little girl had no shortage of imagination. A real Alice in Wonderland.

"You must be starving to death. Do you want something to eat?"

"No. Today I'm not eating."

"What?"

"Some days I don't eat, to give poor people a chance to have something to eat."

Dubuc had heard enough. He took her by the hand and left the room.

"Come on, we're going to find your dear old dad. Poor child, it's not surprising you're nothing but skin and bones. And look at how dirty you are! Jerry is going to have a pretty bad time of it, trust me on that. There are child protection laws, you know."

"I don't want to go see my father! I don't want to!"

Before Dubuc knew it, Sophie had slipped between his legs like a hare, going back into the cupboard where he had found her. He followed her.

"Come back, Sophie!"

Despite repeatedly calling her, he realized that he had lost the little girl. She had escaped by a tiny exit that had been cut through one of the walls. When he tried to follow, his obesity delivered a reality check. His thick haunches forced him to give up the chase.

He went back to the bar and leaned over to one of the waitresses.

"I'm looking for the owner," he said.

She shrugged her shoulders nonchalantly, and continued her rounds, carrying a tray of glasses over her head. Dubuc crossed his arms and rested on his elbows at the bar. Catherine came over to join him.

"Jerry can't be found," he said. "Can you imagine? The little girl has spent the evening in a cupboard."

The next moment, as though leaping out of a musician's tophat, Jerry Ménard came up to them, his arms open wide.

"Well, well, well. What a pleasant surprise! Welcome to the Greluche, Chief Dubuc, and you as well, Mademoiselle. Your throats must be parched. Can I offer you a drink? Nothing at all? All right, I won't insist."

He shook Catherine's hand long enough to make her uncomfortable. Then he went behind the bar to smooth out his black hair, which was stiff with gel, and served himself a cognac before returning to Catherine's side. He seemed to be eating her with his eyes.

"You know, Mademoiselle, I have a weakness for pretty redheads. They have character, and that gets me excited. It's no accident both my ex-wives had red hair."

Catherine managed to keep from laughing in the face of

this self-styled Don Juan who smelled of cheap aftershave. He was floating in a checked suit and staring out at her from behind his glasses.

"How about that! And I thought you'd given up women," said Chief Dubuc.

"I guess they can still get me under their spell, even at my age!" he replied, with a suggestive wink.

He laughed, showing rows of bad teeth, and emptied his glass with a single gulp. Dubuc was standing close enough to him to be able to smell his breath, which was bad enough to strip paint from the walls.

"Do you have any idea where your little girl is right now?"

Ménard remembered the scene in the funeral parlour.

"You're not going to bear a grudge for that all my life, are you? Sophie is like a wind tunnel. She sweeps in and out of rooms. I'm doing the best I can to raise that girl, with what I have to work with, you might say."

"That doesn't say much."

Ménard could see that the police officer wasn't kidding.

"You found her closed up in the cupboard of my office, I bet. It seems as weird to me as it does to you. But what am I supposed to do? Sophie is a little girl who isn't the same as other ones, but she's as clever as a monkey. At four and a half, she already knew how to read and count."

He turned proudly to the crowded room behind him.

"The Greluche has really changed since last time you were here, don't you find?"

The police officer was about to answer when his attention was drawn to a customer of the establishment who had sidled up to Catherine, asking her to dance. Without considering her polite refusal as a real no, he was getting persistent, trying to drag her onto the dance floor. Jerry Ménard hadn't missed a thing. He was quick to react, turning around and snapping his fingers. The next second, the biker was picked up off the floor by two muscular gorillas, who roughly took him out of the building.

Ménard nodded with a self-satisfied look.

"Like I was saying the other day, the Greluche has become a respectable place, Chief Dubuc. You have my word that things will continue this way, as long as I'm at the command."

He turned towards Catherine again, with his broadest smile.

"On behalf of the Greluche, Mademoiselle, I would like to apologize. I can assure you that man will never bother you again."

He snapped his fingers again.

"Gaston, bring a bottle of Dom Pérignon to my office. Three glasses. I've got guests."

Jerry Ménard's two-step tactics were really starting to get on the police officer's nerves.

"Listen, Jerry, we didn't come for this nonsense. I need to have a word with you about J.A., in private."

They followed him to his office. The room was medium-sized. They were met by the smell of sweat that seemed to hang in the air. A ceiling lamp projected a cold, hard light around them. The office was cluttered with empty bottles of alcohol. On the walls, photos of Ménard posing with dancers, a roaming hand reaching for a hip here, a breast there, or else placed firmly on a thigh.

A few minutes later, Ménard poured champagne into the glasses and held the first one out to Catherine, with obvious pleasure. Dubuc couldn't help but notice how quickly the owner of the Greluche had been transformed, in Catherine's presence, from a frog into a Prince Charming. It was probably normal, after all; Jerry Ménard was in home territory now; he had spent his life doing this kind of thing.

"You wanted to talk to me about J.A.?" asked Ménard, sipping his champagne.

"You lied to me like a potion-vendor," retorted the officer. "At the funeral parlour, you stated that you had never had any business dealings with J.A. That's false, and I have proof of it."

He held out a paper to Ménard. "This paper, Jerry, is an agreement between you and J.A., signed a year ago. Bussières committed 150,000 bucks without interest to you, so you could purchase and modernize your Greluche. The contract stipulates, moreover, that in the case of J.A.'s demise, your loan would be cancelled. In other words, you wouldn't owe a bloody cent to anyone. Pretty good deal, I'd say. I am still wondering how you managed to get a suicide clause into your contract with J.A. Everyone knows J.A. was a shark in his business dealings."

Ménard interrupted him with a look full of innuendos.

"You don't understand human nature, Chief Dubuc! Let's say that, between me and J.A., there was a relationship. At one point, we were even pretty close friends."

"Close?" repeated the officer.

The other man looked in Catherine's direction.

"Excuse my frankness, Mademoiselle. You see, J.A. wasn't on very good terms with his wife. As a result, he sometimes needed – how can I put it delicately – a shoulder to cry on."

"And you supplied him with these shoulders, I guess?"

Ménard smiled, as though the answer were obvious. Roméo Dubuc tore the contract out of his hands.

"In eight months, you only paid back peanuts!"

"I put in my best combat effort," the other man replied dryly. "I hope you don't doubt my intentions. Now that business is going better, poor J.A. won't be able to benefit."

The fake air of remorse that Jerry Ménard stuck on his

face didn't fool anybody. Dubuc poured his glass of champagne into the garbage can.

"You can celebrate J.A.'s death alone."

The other man shot him a nasty look.

Dubuc motioned to Catherine that it was time to go. Returning to the car, they could make out moans at the back of the parking lot. They went over on tiptoe. Dubuc grabbed his weapon, as a precaution. Behind a row of trash bins, they saw a man twisted in pain in the grass, his face bloody and his right leg broken below the knee. He had obviously been beaten like a dog. Catherine recognized the biker who had hit on her a little earlier in the Greluche.

Roméo Dubuc swore loudly.

"Jerry has never hesitated to use every means available to achieve his goals. Be careful."

"He's violent?" Catherine asked nervously.

"Violent and sadistic. His two first wives killed themselves. Their bodies were found in a horrendous state. I'll spare you the details. I say 'killed themselves' but, really, several pieces of evidence were doubtful in our investigation. Especially the fact that Jerry was in the area each time. So make me happy, Catherine, will you? Try to forget what happened tonight and stay as far away as possible from that rat-face."

He called the ambulance and leaned over the biker.

"It was Jerry's choir boys who did this to you, eh?"

The other had the troubled expression of a victim who had been through a horrible nightmare. He replied feebly that he had slipped and fallen on the grass.

"Come, come, now! You ended up with your leg broken at the knee? You should bring charges against Ménard, my poor man. We could force him to mow his lawn more often!"

The ambulance drove off in a siren chorus.

"Ménard slipped through my legs once again!" grumbled the police officer. "We missed the perfect opportunity to get him on assault, and question him at the same time about his real business relations with J.A."

★

When Catherine woke up the next morning, the sun had been filtering in for several hours already. The tent was empty. Barbara Watkins had left a note saying that Marie-Ève and she had found a little circus at the other end of the campgrounds. She went over to meet them and join in on the fun.

Marie-Ève pressed up against her.

"You were dreaming all night, Mama."

"Really? Dreaming?" said Catherine, astonished.

Barbara confirmed the truth.

"Yes, you were sitting up and very excited!"

She was going to say something more, but was stopped by a memory of the visit to the Greluche the night before. She had noticed that . . . But it would be better to talk about this in person with Chief Dubuc. She left the girls, promising to be back for supper and hopped into her Jeep.

She had been driving towards Chesterville for fifteen minutes or so when she caught sight of an old, deserted Protestant church in the middle of a field. It was the one Dubuc had told her about. If she wasn't mistaken, this was where his son, André, had died in rather odd circumstances. The little church was in a badly deteriorated condition. A sign with "Private Property" on it had been vandalized.

Catherine parked her Jeep and approached the temple slowly. She didn't have any trouble recognizing, on the outside walls, the satanic messages Chief Dubuc had shown her in his photos. The door, barricaded since the police investigation two years before, had been tampered with in an attempt to break in at least once since then. After a few moments, she had the uncomfortable feeling that she wasn't alone. Her breath quickened and a shiver ran up her spine. She turned around. Her first cousin, J.A. Bussières's son, was standing behind her.

"Conrad!"

Catherine hadn't seen him for several years. The young man – he was in his twenties – facing her now was only a shadow of his former self. His cheeks were drawn and his complexion was pale, making it obvious that he was in a miserable state of health. Catherine couldn't get over the way he trembled.

"Conrad, do you recognize me? I'm your cousin, Catherine. You used to call me 'Cati' when we were young. Do you remember?"

He didn't reply. Catherine noticed his vacant expression. He hadn't taken his medication for several days, and considered her a perfect stranger.

She moved towards him, but he ran off to hide in a corner of the church. He curled up and started moewing like a cat, long, drawn-out moans.

Chief Dubuc arrived at this moment, and walked over to Catherine's side.

"I went to the campgrounds and the girls told me you were coming to see me. I saw your Jeep on the way. Conrad doesn't look very good."

"He's been meowing since I got here. And he's trembling; it's pitiful. Look at him! A gibbering idiot," she said, holding back tears.

"His psychiatrist told me that his condition was very serious. Did you know that he escaped from the hospital the day of your uncle's death?"

"What are you suggesting? Don't be ridiculous! What reason could Conrad have had to kill his father?"

"Hatred. Dr. Rubinsky claims that J.A. had him committed because of Marguerita."

Catherine approached Conrad again. He was still curled up in his corner and meowing ardently. The policeman turned to her.

"We have to get him back to the hospital asap."

He went over to Conrad and grabbed him by the arm. The other man leapt to his feet, turned towards the policeman and dug his nails into the other man's shoulder, letting out a high-pitched scream at the same time. The pain was so sharp that Dubuc released his grip.

"Well, if you want to play dirty, Boy . . . "

The police officer seized Conrad around the waist. But Catherine hurried over to stop him.

"Wait! Do what I do, instead, all right?"

She went over to the opposite side of the room, curled up and began to meow the way Conrad had been doing.

Dubuc couldn't believe his ears.

"Stop these idiotic games!"

"Do what I told you to do."

She resumed her long, plaintive meows under Dubuc's dazed stare. Against his will, the police man forced himself down into a crouch, trying in vain to remember when the last time was that he had put himself in such a ridiculous position.

After a few minutes of the spectacle, Conrad got back up and made his way to Catherine, reaching out for her hand. He did the same with Dubuc. Then he escorted them in silence towards a narrow door at the back of the room that opened into the cellar. They went downstairs a rickety little staircase. The area was dark, dimly lit, and the smell of candle-smoke floated in the air. Roméo Dubuc took out his flashlight. Still astonished by Conrad's strange behaviour, they noticed a little square table up against the wall. It was made of solid oak. At each of the four corners, Catherine noted there was a little metal container with a red substance in it. The police officer, who had wandered off, came back with a silver object.

"I can see this is a chalice, but look how it is dented. It looks like it's been underneath tractor tires!"

Catherine nodded her head, distracted. He could tell she was concentrating on trying to understand what she was looking at in this strange setting.

Conrad had gone back to his refuge in a corner of the cellar, but seemed calmer, now. His eyes followed the slightest movement with rapt attention.

Dubuc pushed aside a few crates that had probably been used as chairs before he found a thick cotton bag. It was dirty and knotted at one end. He picked it up and tried to undo the knot, but it resisted. Quickly reaching the limits of his patience, he took out a pocketknife and cut through the rope. He regretted the impulse immediately. The stench that came out of the bag was such that he closed his eyes and pinched his lips with disgust.

Three dead cats were decomposing.

Dubuc swore, closed the sack and threw it as far away from himself as he could.

"Feeling better?" asked Catherine.

"Tell me what's happening to us. Is this a nightmare, or what?"

She led the police officer off to one side and lowered her voice.

"It was here that André died, wasn't it?"

"I already said so."

Catherine nodded. She chose her words carefully.

"We're in a place where they perform Black Mass."

Chief Dubuc stared at her with a stunned expression, his eyes popping out of his face.

"Come here. I want to show you something," she said.

They went back over to the low table they had noticed when they came in.

"I'm not an expert in satanism," said Catherine, "but as far as I'm concerned, two plus two always equals four. See this little table up against the wall? It's facing west. That's typical of altars used for satanic rituals."

"But that isn't enough to . . . "

"Let me finish. Now, look at the four corners of the table. Notice anything?"

"Well, there are three little copper plates with leftover bits of red wax, it looks like."

He touched it with his finger and brought it to his lips to check.

"Exactly. It's red wax. Satanic cults often use red candles to invoke the powers of hell. I have the feeling that we are dealing with a pretty specific group of people, here, Chief Dubuc. Have you ever heard of the Cult of the Cat?"

"Never. Is it a new heavy metal group?"

"Don't be cynical. The Cult of the Cat is a satanic cult that is pretty well known in the United States and in some countries in Central America. As far as I can tell, the group was started at the beginning of the century in Guadalajara, Mexico. Its members have been performing ritual sacrifices for a long time now, sacrificing small animals, especially cats. They meet in secret, usually at the time of the full moon. They believe that by eating the flesh of the animals they sacrifice and drinking their blood they will have eternal life. It's a belief inspired by ancient Aztec traditions."

The officer shook his head.

"Let's be serious for a few seconds, Catherine. Who would be so stupid that they would eat a dead cat cut up in little pieces and drink its blood? To do that, my dear lady, you would have to be on a pretty bad acid trip."

Catherine shared his disgust.

"I'm with you. The very thought that people could practise this kind of ritual makes me sick. But we have to be realistic. These Black Masses are taking place. Look around you: the orientation of the table, the red candles, the desecrated vase, animals that have been sacrificed – they're all signs that don't lie."

Roméo Dubuc tried to quiet his own anxiety.

"All right. Let's say that it's true. The police can't intervene to prevent them from meeting and practising their religion. You know as well as I do that there are laws in this country protecting freedom of religion."

"If that's all it is," said Catherine. "At its beginnings, in Mexico, the Cult of the Cat was pretty 'harmless.' Its members were satisfied with sacrificing small animals by fire. But certain cults inspired by their rituals have started to kidnap children and even committed murder. As you know, that's a long way from freedom of belief."

Conrad, still sitting in his corner, had started up his meowing again, reminding the officer that there were more urgent matters at hand.

"Meanwhile, we have to get your cousin back to the hospital. We can't leave him here, like this. He's so pathetic, it breaks my heart."

When they got Conrad Bussières back to the Chesterville Psychiatric Hospital, it caused quite a ruckus on the third floor. Dr. Rubinsky ordered a comprehensive series of tests, prepared his medications and made sure his patient had a good meal.

"How did you find him?" he asked.

"Just by chance," said Dubuc. "He was hiding out in the old Protestant church near the Chesterville exit. He really isn't doing well. Look at how he's shaking like a leaf."

"That's one of the side effects of the anti-psychotic he

has to take. Long-term, the medication leads to tardive dyskinesia, the same kind of trembling as in Parkinson's. Have you had a chance to question him about his father's death?"

"Conrad is in no state to talk, as you can see," Dubuc answered. "But he probably witnessed some disturbing events recently, and I'd like to be able to question him as soon as possible. Take care of him like he's the apple of your eye, Dr. Rubinsky. And call me as soon as he gets better."

Chapter 7

Catherine Gagnon arrived just as Chief Dubuc finished sprinkling a generous quantity of herbs and spices on a gigantic portion of shepherd's pie.

"You're eating again?"

When it came to comments about his appetite, the policeman could get pretty defensive.

"Not you too!"

Seeing that she had pushed one of his buttons, Catherine changed the subject as quickly as she could.

"Would you mind if I made a call to the United States?"

"Be my guest."

"I want to talk to Howard Sinclair about what we discovered in the old, abandoned church."

"And who would this gentleman be?"

"An American expert on cults. Howard has written several books about satanism and has even served as an advisor to the FBI. I've met him at sociology conferences. He teaches at the University of Atlanta, in Georgia."

The police officer could tell that Catherine had reached her American colleague when the conversation switched into English. He left the room and came back when Catherine had finished her call.

"Bad news. According to Howard, the Cult of the Cat is thought to be an American cult that is quite active in several Canadian provinces, including Alberta, Saskatchewan and Québec. The FBI is apparently in close contact with the RCMP and the Sûreté du Québec."

"How do we know we're not dealing with your average, run-of-the-mill cat-killers?"

"It's more serious than that. I described to Howard the

objects that we found in the cellar of the old church, and he says there's no doubt in his mind. It's a true satanic cult. It sounds to him like it's a lot like the Cult of the Cat in the U.S.A. Some members seem to have dissociated themselves from the main one to form other cults that are more violent. They go as far as to sexually abuse children and even make human sacrifices."

"I'm going to have to keep an eye on the old church, that's for sure." announced Dubuc.

"According to Howard, you'd better not waste any time. As soon as the members of the cult have performed a few satanic masses in one place, they move on to another one really quickly to get everyone off their trail."

"But the objects they left are proof they're intending to come back, aren't they?"

"Maybe they were. But now that they know we've found their little hiding place, they're likely to take off pretty fast."

The officer was intrigued.

"You say they know?" he grimaced, puzzled. "Cripes! How could these people possibly know unless they followed us?"

"Howard claims it's the case. The members in this cult have eyes and ears everywhere. The believers know every move the police make. You said so yourself. Everybody in Chesterville knows what everyone else is doing."

★

The next morning, Marguerita Bussières was surprised to find Chief Dubuc at her door. She was wearing a light negligee that she wrapped around herself modestly.

"I got your message, but I wasn't expecting you so early.

Give me five minutes to get dressed. Have a seat in the living room, I'll be right with you."

She came back dressed in a grey suit and matching pumps.

"I'm sorry I'm disturbing you so early in the morning," apologized the policeman.

"No problem," answered J.A.'s widow, sweeping away any objections with the back of her hand. "Would you like some coffee?"

She left the room and came back with two delicate porcelain cups. As he went to place his cup on the little table beside him, Dubuc carelessly knocked an ashtray onto the carpet.

"Oh, what a klutz!" he said, jumping up. "Bring me a cloth, would you? I'll wipe it up for you. I've got all those ashes and cigarette butts on your beautiful Persian carpet. My wife is right when she says I'm like a bull in a china shop."

When Marguerita Bussières came back with the cloth, she was surprised to find the chief of police on his hands and knees on the carpet, doing what he could to tidy up the mess.

She burst out laughing.

"Now, now, don't fuss. I was going to get rid of the carpet anyway. My housekeeper is coming over in an hour. She'll clean it up."

Dubuc apologized profusely and sat down again. A big white cat jumped onto his knees, moewing loudly.

"How are you coping?"

"With J.A.'s death? Just between you and me, I was pretty much accustomed to his absence. He was very busy with his business affairs, which I have to look after now. Just yesterday I got a letter from the regional branch of the Canadian Mental Health Association. They're asking me to serve as the president of their next fund-raising campaign. I'll gladly accept their invitation, because of Conrad's state."

"I see you're not going to have time on your hands."

"They say keeping busy keeps your mind off your own problems. But you didn't come to talk about my volunteer work, I'm sure."

"You mentioned Conrad. How is he doing?"

"Poor child," sighed Marguerita, getting up.

She picked up a framed photo of J.A.'s son from the table beside her and handed it to Chief Dubuc.

"This boy is the reason his father got up in the morning. I often told J.A. that he should have sent him to a specialized facility, you know, where he could have better care than in a little hole in the ground like Chesterville."

"You don't like this area?" the officer asked coldly.

"Oh, it isn't a value judgment, Chief Dubuc. But serious illnesses can't be treated properly in a regional hospital. I had a difficult childhood and I don't accept other people's misery easily. That might be why I have so much affection for Conrad."

"And yet, if I'm to believe what people say, you didn't like him much."

Marguerita Bussières shifted her hips slightly on the chesterfield. Dubuc noticed that the index finger of her right hand suddenly stopped stirring the little silver coffeespoon in her cup.

"That is false."

He could tell she was lying.

"Gossip is one of the things I could never stand about Chesterville. Believe me, I am even more attached than ever since J.A.'s death. That child is all that I still have of my dear, dead husband."

"And money, of course," added the policeman, pushing the cat away so that he could get up.

Marguerita darted a nasty look at him.

"What are you insinuating?"

"I don't really like to have to say it, but your husband's death must have left you with quite a pile of money. According to the notary public, J.A. left you almost two million dollars in his will."

She stood up and turned her back on the police officer, who could barely make out her voice, rough and on the verge of tears.

"How can you calculate the importance of J.A.'s death in terms of money? Have you no heart, Chief Dubuc?"

The officer stood up and walked over to place his hand on her shoulder.

"I share your sorrow. Sincerely. But your husband has been killed and I need to find out who's guilty. It's my job and I am going to do everything in my power to do it. In your case, the money is more than sufficient grounds to get rid of J.A. After all, he left you a small fortune, enough to live like Zsa Zsa Gabor until the end of your days, isn't that right?"

"I like money, Chief Dubuc. That much is true. My family was as poor as church mice and I swore that I would do well for myself, that I would never be broke again. But I wouldn't kill my husband for more."

"Maybe not, but I can't dismiss the possibility of vengeance, either, the punishment of a woman who had been cheated on for many years by a man who spent his time gallivanting and chasing skirts."

"Am I a suspect?"

"Let's say you're on my list of people to visit."

"I imagine you want to know where I was at the time the crime was committed."

"You've read my mind."

"As I said, the other day at the Police Station, I was

visiting my sister in Sherbrooke. When I got home, I took a hot bath and I went to bed, without waiting for J.A. He always got in late."

"Who can attest to your version of the facts?"

"All you have to do is call my sister."

"Here, in Chesterville! Who can confirm that you were in bed at eleven-thirty p.m., the approximate time of the murder?"

"No one, I'm afraid."

"In that case, you've got a bit of a problem."

Marguerita Bussières looked at him with a worried look.

"What are you insinuating?"

"I'm trying to figure out who, in J.A.'s circles, would have had a sufficient motive to murder him. When you came to the office, the other day, you gave the impression of being a reserved woman, in control of herself, and very capable of getting her own way if she wanted something."

Bussières's widow approached the policeman and sat down next to him, calmer this time.

"Can you keep a secret?"

The officer's face twisted with annoyance. "I'm not a priest. I'm investigating a crime."

"I'm going to tell you anyway. I wasn't alone at the time of the murder."

"Well, well! And who were you with?"

To the amazement of the policeman, she replied:

"I was in bed with Roland Fafard, J.A.'s chauffeur."

★

"Okay, Girls, everybody to the table! Lunch is served!" called Catherine.

Marie-Ève, Barbara and Sophie rushed in, out of breath,

while Coconut the cat ran behind them. Sophie stayed off to one side.

"Come on, Sophie!" shouted Marie-Ève. "Mama has some for you too. It's spaghetti."

The little girl came in, taking tiny steps forward, her face lowered and observing Catherine attentively out of the corner of her eye. Her eyes were bright blue and rather baleful. She smiled at her. The outline of her body under her dirty and inexpensive dress was extremely thin. Before the meal, she picked up a piece of cheese with her fingertips and ate it slowly, still watching Catherine. Later, the three girls returned to their games.

Early in the afternoon, Catherine suggested that they take a boat ride on the Lac des Sables, a suggestion that was met with hoots of joy. She sat down on the bench in the middle and rowed slowly. The boat edged along the shoreline at a lazy pace. Out in the distance, they could see stretches of pastureland. The farms perched here and there gave the impression of being part of a Swiss landscape.

Catherine had lost the habit of this kind of exercise. She soon turned around and headed back to the campground. The boat passed a small animal that was struggling to swim to the other shore.

"Mama, look! There's a big fat cat trying to reach land!" cried Marie-Ève.

"It's a muskrat! A muskrat!" Barbara shouted in English.

Catherine looked around quickly. It was, indeed, a muskrat.

"Faster! Faster!" Marie-Ève cried out again and again. Her excitement was reaching a peak.

But Catherine had noticed that the appearance of the animal had provoked quite a different reaction from Sophie Ménard. The little girl was glued to her seat and seemed petrified. Catherine passed the oars to Barbara and tried to take Sophie in her arms, but she slipped away and huddled at the bottom of the boat. Her whole body was trembling like a leaf.

Catherine motioned to Barbara to take the boat back to shore right away, despite Marie-Ève's continuing protests.

*

The heat at the end of the afternoon was slowly falling when the patrol car narrowly missed a bicycle-rider crossing the main street. Chief Dubuc braked abruptly, turned off the ignition and sponged the sweat off his forehead. He got out of the car, tried in vain to apologize to the unfortunate cyclist, took a couple of deep breaths and a few steps along the sidewalk. Somewhat calmer, he got back in behind the wheel and continued on to the Police Station. Lucien, who was busy compiling monthly statistics on criminal activity in Chesterville, noticed his nervousness.

"I nearly took the head off a guy who was trying to cross Main Street on his bike!" thundered Dubuc. "A second later and crack!"

"Weren't you paying attention?"

"I was literally on another planet, my dear man. I went to visit Marguerita early this morning. I had to check some information and I backed her up against a wall. She admitted that, at the time of the crime, she was in the arms of – guess who? None other than Roland Fafard."

"J.A.'s chauffeur? That's not possible," declared the deputy, getting back to his work.

"Why not?" asked Dubuc.

"I thought that Roland was . . . "

"Was what?"

"You know what I mean!"

"Well, me too. I always thought that Roland was more interested in men. But that's not Marguerita's opinion. Let's see. I wrote it down here. 'Roland gave me the best sex I've had since my honeymoon.' That's what she said."

"Pshaw! And you believe her story?"

"You know me. I just wanted to go to the source. Fafard turned as red as a tomato, and when he found out I'd talked to Marguerita, he spilled the beans and admitted he was in bed with his boss at the time of the crime. Their affair had apparently only been going on for a month. Marguerita had it up to her eyeballs with J.A. stepping out on her, and said she was going to get back at him."

"You seem sceptical," ventured the deputy.

"Good golly! You know as well as I do that Fafard has been working for J.A. for twenty years. Now Marguerita's his boss. That woman can make him say anything she wants. Fafard is like a puppet. It's too bad for him; Marguerita's going to keep pulling the strings."

"He'd lie to keep his job?"

"And to provide an alibi for Marguerita. We're going to have to find something better than that, my dear man."

★

At the beginning of the evening, Chief Dubuc was about to leave the office when he caught sight of Catherine's unmistakable red hair in the staircase.

"Going somewhere?" she asked.

"Nowhere important. I was just going to watch a baseball game on TV. My wife's gone to play cards with her girlfriends. For me, bridge."

"You prefer poker. It's more exciting."

He watched her smile at him as she leaned against the doorframe.

"With a smile like that, I bet you have something up your sleeve. You're really J.A.'s niece after all, aren't you?"

She laughed. "Ever since I spoke to Howard, I can't help thinking . . . I've got a thousand questions about what the cult might have been up to in the cellar of the church. I would've liked to see whether Conrad could remember something, anything. Do you think we could go and see him?"

"You think your cousin knows something we don't?"

"Don't forget – Conrad was hiding in that abandoned church for quite a while. He's the one who led us to the cellar where the cult performs its Black Mass rituals. The chances are good that he saw or heard something interesting. We have nothing to lose by asking him some questions."

"I like your idea, but we'll have to check with Rubinsky. He'll have to give us permission to see him. I haven't heard from him since we took the patient back."

⋆

At the hospital, the two went up and down a series of long, deserted and unfriendly corridors until they got to Stanley Rubinsky's office. The door was ajar. Roméo Dubuc coughed. The psychiatrist raised his head.

"Oh, come in, Chief Dubuc."

"How is Conrad?"

"We're still doing our assessment. One of my colleagues thinks he may have a permanent skull fracture."

"Would it be possible to see him?"

"Maybe next week."

"Tonight. We want to see him right away."

"Is it that urgent?" asked the psychiatrist, surprised.

"I have to question him for my investigation. Every minute counts."

"In that case, follow me."

The doctor led them to a small, dim room with large mirrors and carpeting on the walls.

"One-way mirrors," commented Dubuc, touching the glass with his fingertip. "They can watch us from the other side."

"Shall I go ahead?" Catherine asked.

"If you like."

Conrad appeared a few seconds later, flanked by an orderly who stayed outside the room. The police officer motioned to him to sit down and joined Catherine on the other side of the table. She walked towards Conrad, making her way along the wall, and put her hand on Conrad's.

"Conrad, it's me, Catherine. Do you recognize me? Cati."

Conrad remained silent. He was scruffy and didn't look well. His eyes were fixed on the table in front of him. After a moment, which seemed to last for centuries, his hand eventually reached out to shake Catherine's.

"Cati . . . "

It was as though his brain was making superhuman efforts to cross through the thick fog his anti-psychotic medication had created.

He seemed to remember. Catherine continued:

"Conrad, do you remember the old church?"

"Old church . . . "

He repeated the words mechanically, trying to make sense of them.

"The church," said Catherine. "The cellar of the church. Try to remember, it's important."

Chief Dubuc whispered in Catherine's ear:

"Given the smell of candle-smoke that still hung in the air, I'd say the ceremony had taken place the night before. We need to know if Conrad was hiding there."

"Six . . . " Conrad suddenly said.

"Six what?" asked Catherine.

"Six in the cellar."

"Did you see them?" jumped in Dubuc.

"With black capes," he said in a voice that was pasty and heavy with medication.

"Were you hiding in the church?"

"Hiding. Down in the cellar."

His hand abruptly let Catherine's slip out. He seemed to have quickly fallen into a vegetative state."

"Do something, Catherine. We can't lose him again!"

Desperate, Catherine took out of her pocket the little black cat. She placed it on the table in front of Conrad.

The sight of the object seemed to revive his memory. He took it into his hands.

"Chingon, the Grand Chingon . . . He's the leader."

"The leader of the cult is named The Grand Chingon?" asked Dubuc.

"He summoned a little girl . . . dressed all in white . . . flowers in her hair . . . the others were watching . . . "

"Do you know who she is?" asked Catherine.

"The little girl is Satan's bride."

On hearing these words, Roméo Dubuc got up from the table and started to pace nervously.

"A little girl! I should have guessed!"

Catherine signalled to him that he needed to calm down.

"Go on, Conrad."

He started to get upset and began to tremble.

"The Grand Chingon asked her to climb onto the altar. Everyone was kneeling down in front of the little girl. Everyone, with red candles. They were chanting. And then . . . "

"Then what?" asked Dubuc, impatient.

"Then he held the little girl in his arms. And then he laid her down on the altar . . . Then he moved her legs apart."

Conrad got up, trembling violently. He was unable to continue.

"And he . . . "

Conrad shook his head.

"The little girl screamed! She was screaming!"

Conrad gripped his head between his two hands and screamed with fright.

Chief Dubuc pushed Catherine out of the room.

"Quick! Get help!"

The orderly entered, followed by Dr. Rubinsky. They injected a sedative into Conrad's arm, and he collapsed on the spot.

The doctor shook his head in disapproval.

"It's my fault! I shouldn't have left you alone with him. What stupidity! What did you do to him?"

Dubuc didn't know what to say.

"I needed some details for my investigation, and I'm afraid I pushed him too far. The memory of certain events was obviously too painful for Conrad. It upset him. I'm sorry."

Without meeting their eyes, the doctor gestured to them to leave the room. Two orderlies carried Conrad out, motionless.

Conrad and Dubuc looked at each other without saying anything, and waited until they were outside the hospital before they opened their mouths.

"Can you imagine! If what Conrad says is true, he must have witnessed the rape of a little girl by a cult. Stan Rubinsky warned us, though, that he tends to be delirious because of the effects of the medicine. Who knows? He could have been hearing imaginary voices. Is it possible, Catherine? In the mind of a poor mental patient like him, how can we tell where the truth ends and delirium begins?"

Catherine stopped short and looked the police officer in the eye.

"As far as I'm concerned, it isn't simply a case of pure delusion. Conrad's description of the satanic ceremony stands up very well to everything I know about it. There's the sexual sacrifice of the young virgin, the priest called the Grand Chingon, the red candles . . . everything that we usually find in satanic worship rituals in groups like the Cult of the Cat.

When they got back to the patrol car, they found Lucien Langlois slumped over the hood of the car, trying to get his breath.

"Where the heck were you?" he finally managed to get out, panting and fanning his shirt, which was soaking wet.

"In there!" said Dubuc, pointing to the hospital.

His deputy was clutching his chest with both hands.

"I looked everywhere for you!"

"You didn't have to run all the way over here! You're not Ben Johnson, you know. Couldn't it wait?"

Lucien shook his head.

"We found the weapon used in the crime. The murderer's knife," announced the deputy triumphantly. "With J.A.'s blood all over the blade!"

Before Dubuc could open his mouth, Lucien gave him the answer he was waiting so impatiently for.

"It belongs to Jules Talbot."

Chapter 8

Decaying rubbish was spread out as far as the eye could see, and the damp morning heat seemed to make the smell even more powerful. Even the sign for the Chesterville Landfill Site had been unable to resist the onslaught of starving rats. Roméo Dubuc leaned over towards his deputy, sniffling noisily.

"What a mess! It's a pretty weird idea to hold a press conference in a garbage dump, wouldn't you say? The stench is enough to peel the skin off my nostrils!"

"The mayor thought it would be fitting, since it was an employee of the sanitation department that found the weapon used in the crime."

"Oh, come on! The real reason was that Marc-Yvon wants to build up the ammunition in his darn dump is so he can get the dough he needs to enlarge it. He's no fool, that Beaudette. He knows that all the media contacts will be here this morning."

Marc-Yvon Beaudette raised his arms in the air, asking the fifteen or so people present to be silent.

"My friends, I will now ask the Chief of Police, Mr. Roméo Dubuc, to say a few words so that we will learn about the latest developments in the Bussières case."

Dubuc walked by some of the big-wigs of the village and made his way to the front. A few metres away from him was Marguerita Bussières, accompanied by her chauffeur, Roland Fafard.

The police officer turned towards the two photographers who were there and flashed a butcher knife stained with red and wrapped in a plastic bag. Camera flashes caught his every move.

One of the reporters came forward.

"Bernard Caron, from the *St. Stéphane Progress*. Chief Dubuc, is this really the weapon used in the crime?"

"Yes, my friend. The lab gave us the results no more than an hour ago. The analysis proved that the dry blood on the blade was A negative, the same type as the victim's."

"The weapon was found here?" asked a voice.

"Right here," answered Dubuc, pointing his finger behind him. "The knife was hidden under a pile of trash."

"Have you determined where the weapon came from?" continued Bernard Caron.

"The knife belonged to Jules Talbot, a grocer from Chesterville. I should add that Talbot's been a suspect since the beginning of our investigation and that there was no love lost between him and the victim. As you can see, it's an ordinary butcher knife with a wooden handle, except that here, at the extremity, we can read the initials "JT" which stand for Jules Talbot, carved in it. At this point in our investigation, we can confirm that the knife is one of the utensils used by the suspect every day in the course of his work. Moreover, he confirmed that fact himself when he was arrested and questioned last night."

"What's the motive for the crime?" asked Jeannot Lejeune, continuing to take photos all over the place.

"Revenge. Pure and simple revenge," answered Dubuc. "The examination of the scene of the crime revealed that theft was not the motive. At the time of his death, Monsieur Bussières had at least $5,400 on his person, as well as a Rolex watch that was worth at least twice that amount. However, his murderer did not touch that. He was killed out of revenge. Jules Talbot knew that the victim was in love with his daughter, and he was afraid he would get her pregnant. He had already threatened to settle the score in front of witnesses. We also have testimony that Talbot has a fiery disposition, acts impulsively and has already been implicated in a number of incidents."

"Has he confessed?" asked Bernard Caron.

The policeman hesitated before replying.

"We questioned Jules Talbot for three hours last night, without getting a confession. He continues to claim that he had nothing to do with the murder, that someone stole the butcher knife from his store and so on and so forth. The interrogation will continue today."

"Is it possible that he's innocent?" asked Caron.

"Innocent? Judge for yourself: his fingerprints are all over the knife!" exploded Dubuc, waving the weapon around again.

Lejeune, in his corner, could be heard croaking:

"It's unbelievable! The police have the murderer, the weapon, fingerprints, the motive, but no confession. What a great job they're doing!"

Dubuc suddenly felt an intolerable urge to make the man swallow dandelion root, but he managed to control himself.

"That's about where we're at for the moment, Monsieur Lejeune," he concluded.

*

Catherine came back to the campground late in the afternoon and was surprised to find Barbara Wilkins there by herself, getting supper ready.

"Where's Marie-Ève?" she asked in English.

"She's playing with Sophie near the pond."

Catherine hurried over towards the pond, after quickly chastising Barbara for having let a little six-year-old girl out of her sight, especially near water. Barely into the woods, Catherine could already make out Marie-Ève and

Sophie Ménard, standing up in a boat about thirty metres away, shouting and playing with great amusement. She got there just in time to see Sophie lose her footing, scream and fall into the water. Catherine rushed over to her, wading through the water that was up to her knees, and got the little girl back up on her feet.

"Would you mind telling me exactly what this game is all about, Girls?" Catherine told them off.

"We wanted to jump off the other board, but Sophie fell into the water," sobbed Marie-Ève.

Catherine brought the girls back to the tent and found them some dry clothes. Sophie quickly ran off to find refuge under a tree and began to weep.

"Papa is going to be mad I got my clothes wet!"

And her sobs started again, even more loudly this time.

Without a word, Catherine crouched down at the same level as the little girl and took her in her arms, which seemed to console her a little bit. Then she led her back into the tent, took off her soaking clothes and put one of Marie-Ève's dresses on her. Although she was four years older than Marie-Ève, Sophie wore the same size as the younger girl, because she was so thin. Catherine noticed that the bones of her rib-cage stood out just under the surface of her skin.

"Here we are, some nice dry clothes for you, Sophie. Hurry over to the table now. Supper is about to be served, and the others are waiting for you."

Roméo Dubuc arrived shortly after the meal and was surprised to find Catherine a little ways off, looking preoccupied and reserved.

"The girls told me I could find you here."

"I needed to be alone for a while," she said, pensively, leaning up against a tree trunk.

Her head was still lowered and her index finger traced out an evasive circle on the sandy ground.

"What do you know about Jerry Ménard's daughter?"

"Sophie? Not much. Her mother was a dancer who took off when she was born. Jerry's been taking care of her in his own style, dragging the little girl into clubs with him, that sort of thing. Why do you ask?"

Catherine looked up.

"That child is not normal, Chief. And I'm not just talking about her emotional state. You've noticed just as I have. She nearly dies of fright every time an adult goes near her. And her physical health is terrible; it worries me. Have you seen the tips of her fingers? They're bent like an old woman's, as though the bones have been broken. Sophie is undernourished, that's obvious. And then there are the red marks . . . "

"What red marks?"

"Around her vulva. I saw them when I changed her clothes a few minutes ago. When I touched her by mistake, Sophie stiffened up. I'm convinced that the child has been sexually abused. I'd swear it. We have to do something."

The police officer scratched his head, as though hesitating in the face of the inevitable.

"Sexual abuse – that's easy to say. I know Jerry is capable of anything, but even so. It's like everyone on the whole planet is victim of sexual abuse these days. What if it's just an allergy that's caused the red marks?"

Catherine leapt up.

"Good Lord! As a mother, I am quite capable of recognizing signs like these when I see them! Whether it's my daughter or someone else's, I can tell!"

Seeing her determination, Dubuc withdrew his objections.

"What do you suggest then?"

"That we take her to the hospital right away for a complete examination. They'll probably have a psychologist or a psychiatrist see her."

"We'll have to inform Jerry. After all, she's his daughter."

"Judging by her condition, Sophie must be the last thing he worries about. We'll get in touch with him when the little girl is safe. Come on, let's go."

*

Roméo Dubuc got back from the hospital in the early afternoon and hurried into his office. A package wrapped in a brown manilla bag was waiting for him on his desk. He didn't have to open it to know what it was: the smell of hot meat loaf filled the whole basement. His mouth watering with eagerness, he sat down at the table as soon as he had closed his door. Eating was, for him, a ritual that he carried out with care and an incredible, almost fanatical seriousness. Let anyone who dared interrupt the ceremony be wary. Jeannot Lejeune had learned this the hard way.

The policeman had almost finished his meal when the telephone rang. He hesitated a moment, but his sense of duty carried the day. He picked up the receiver. It was the coroner, Ernest Moreau.

"You have a talent for calling me when my mouth's full. Sorry. I didn't mean anything by it. I've almost finished anyway."

"In case you're interested," explained the coroner, "I've had the autopsy report on J.A. Bussières's body reviewed by one of my colleagues in Montréal. He did some more extensive analyses of the angle at which the knife penetrated the victim's rib cage. Your murderer is, indeed, right-handed. Were you aware of that?"

"That corresponds with what we know about Talbot."

"Speaking of that, have you ever heard of ATP?" asked the coroner.

"ATP? Isn't that the Association of Tennis Professionals?"

The laugh of the old doctor at the other end of the line let him know he was wrong.

"Actually, no. ATP is the abbreviation for adenosine triphosphate, a chemical compound involved in the transfer of energy that takes place in live cells."

"Is that important for me to know?" Dubuc ventured, despite his horror of scientific jargon.

The coroner hesitated for a moment.

"That all depends," Moreau continued. "It's your investigation, Roméo, not mine. I'm just trying to help you as best I can."

"Go on then," said Dubuc, more out of politeness than anything else.

"Fine. I need to say that the autopsy revealed a significant decrease in the level of ATP in Bussières's organism. That's interesting, because it implies a transfer of cellular energy of some importance took place just before he died. Are you still with me? Basically, we can deduce that there is a strong chance Bussières had been running to escape from his assailant."

"Well, well!" said the policeman, suddenly interested. "And yet we found no trace of a struggle on Bussières's body. You made that statement yourself at the time of the autopsy. Nothing except slight scratches on the shoulders. It's as though Bussières just let himself be stabbed without blinking an eyelash!"

"I'll repeat what I just said. It's quite likely that he tried to escape from his murderer by running away, which would explain the noticeable drop in the ATP levels in his organism," stated the coroner.

Roméo Dubuc had dropped his fork to pick up a pen. He listened to Dr. Moreau's explanations with great interest.

"Duly noted, Doc. Thank you for your information."

Roméo Dubuc remained sitting silently at his desk for a

long while, thinking things over, reading and rereading his notes.

★

Catherine and Marie-Ève were sitting at a picnic table near the canteen. The little girl hadn't touched her plate and had a sad look on her face.

"Come on, Marie-Ève, you have to eat *something* at least."

The child grimaced.

"I know," Catherine said, gently touching her hand. "You're worried about your friend Sophie, is that it? Never mind, the doctors will examine her and she'll probably be back soon."

"Why do the doctors have to examine her?" asked Marie-Ève.

"Because someone hurt her," said Catherine.

"It wasn't me, Mama! I didn't hurt Sophie!" the little girl began to shout.

Catherine pulled her daughter over to her and held her in her arms.

"No, of course not, Darling, I know it wasn't you. You're a good friend to Sophie."

Seeing that Marie-Ève was starting to cry, Catherine decided to head back. On their way over to the Jeep, she realized she didn't have her keys.

She quickly went back to the table, hunting in the grass with her toes. Nothing. Remembering suddenly that she had left them on the seat of the car, she returned calmly to the Jeep. Nothing.

She tried to get her thoughts straight so she wouldn't panic. Barbara Watkins had a duplicate, but she had stayed at the campground. Catherine was going to the telephone booth near the canteen when a big black Plymouth with tinted-glass windows suddenly appeared. The passenger window was rolled down and the driver gestured in Catherine's direction.

"Did you lose something, my red-haired lovely?"

She heard a metallic clink.

Jerry Ménard was jingling her key ring around in his hand. She went over to him.

"Climb in. The little one too."

Catherine refused outright.

"Okay. Too bad for your keys then, my dear." Ménard got ready to take off.

"No, wait! I'll come."

Catherine buckled Marie-Ève into the back seat and sat down in the front, beside Ménard. With a loud and abrupt noise, all the car doors locked. Jerry Ménard turned the steering wheel sharply and the Plymouth took off down the road, tires screeching.

"Where are we going?" asked Catherine, frightened and furious at the same time.

"Never fear, Jerry is here," said Ménard in his nasal voice. "We're just going for a little ride in the neighbourhood. I wanted to talk to you without your big moustached mutt barking at me. He's been sticking to me like flypaper."

Catherine couldn't tell whether Ménard was talking that way because he was jealous or simply cautious.

In the car, the air smelled of the same fragrance of cheap aftershave as there was when she met Ménard for the first time. The interior of the Plymouth was tastelessly decorated: the seats were covered by a bright orange plush dust cover and a rubber doll with bare breasts hanging from the rear-view mirror shook every time the road got bumpy. Jerry Ménard definitely felt like he was in charge. He chewed on a cigar with a satisfied air. He quickly turned off Route 218 onto a deserted country road. Catherine felt fear invade her. She closed her eyes and, for the first time in many years, she murmured a prayer.

The car rolled along the road for ten minutes or so before it reached a clearing. Jerry Ménard stopped the car and told them to get out. He then ordered them to walk in front of him. The trio got to the other side of the clearing and were swallowed by a damp, dense brush. Catherine and Marie-Ève walked hand-in-hand down the muddy trail, followed by Ménard. Catherine wished she could run away, but her legs were shaky and weak and her heart was pumping wildly. They soon reached a second clearing, much smaller than the other one, and she saw, to her dismay, a dozen grey gravestones nearly overtaken by vegetation. Ménard went up to one of them and stood there, pensive, for a moment. Then, as if he was afraid of cracking, he turned around.

"That's Sophie's mother," he said, simply. "This is where our dear parish of Chesterville made it a habit to store the leftovers of the village. Lucille died from an overdose of coke. Suicide. The little girl has never been told that part of it. She thinks her mother went back to the city."

Then, as though the little pilgrimage had enabled him to make peace with himself, Ménard reassembled his everyday look of disdain.

"Mind your own bloody business, Catherine! Sophie's my kid, and I'll raise her as I see fit. She doesn't need to go to the hospital for care."

"But Sophie has problems," said Catherine.

"Shut up!" screamed Ménard. "You think you're smart. A college prof. Who do you think you are, sending my daughter to the hospital? Sophie isn't a nut case, she's very intelligent. She's just too sensitive. She's like a flower about to open. Sometimes I get the impression she's going to turn out like a rose, but other days, it's like she's going to get stepped on. My daughter is all that's left that's mine in this world, and nobody's going to get between her and me. Nobody – get it?"

Ménard suddenly went up to Marie-Ève and caressed her blond curls slowly and tenderly. His nasty grin petrified Catherine.

"Your daughter is beautiful. Watch out for her."

Catherine held Marie-Ève's trembling hand, dreading the thought that, in the next second, Ménard might decide to get revenge. But after a quarter of an hour, he signalled to them to return to the car. On the way back, Ménard was quiet. When they reached the parking lot beside the canteen, he handed her back her keys. They heard the click of the doors of the Plymouth that told them they were free once again.

Catherine took Marie-Ève in her arms and walked quickly to her Jeep. Ménard's nasal voice echoed behind her and sent a shiver up her spine. She turned around. He was smiling at her.

"I'll see you later, my lovely. Women like you excite me."

Chapter 9

"Ménard did *what?*"

Roméo Dubuc leapt to his feet and hammered his fist on his desk in rage.

"I am going to twist that bastard's neck!"

"Oh, calm down," Catherine repeated yet again.

She had never seen the police officer throw such a tantrum.

"The rotten rat-face! Didn't I warn you? Do you have any idea how risky that was?"

"I was scared, and Marie-Ève was too. That's true. But Ménard didn't have any evil ideas. When he got to his wife's grave, he took out his handkerchief and I even thought he was going to cry."

"Cry? Don't kid yourself. Jerry has fewer tears than a crocodile!"

Catherine made a face.

"So I guess I behaved like a moron."

Faced with her reaction, Dubuc changed his tone.

"Listen, don't hold it against me. I just wanted to warn you. You and the girls have to keep your distance. Jerry is a funny son of a gun. I already told you that both his wives died in rather bizarre circumstances and he wasn't far off either time. I thought that would convince you to avoid him like the plague."

"I had no choice!" retorted Catherine, on the verge of tears. "Ménard was dangling my keys under my nose, laughing like a madman! What would you have done in my place?"

She sat down again, plunging her face into her hands, and sobbed quietly under the dismayed gazes of Chief

Dubuc and Marie-Ève. They sensed she needed to empty the tension under which her unexpected encounter with Jerry Ménard had placed her. But the police officer couldn't stand tears. In such moments, he always pictured his own mother, leaning over his father, a policeman, gunned down in an alley when he was still just a boy. He went out of the room to make some coffee.

Catherine joined him a quarter of an hour later.

Dubuc was uncomfortable. He held her cup out to her with a nervous hand.

"It's over now," remarked Catherine, wiping her eyes and pasting a forced smile on her lips.

She sat Marie-Ève on her lap.

"Anything new on Talbot?" she asked, to change the subject.

"Not really. We may have the weapon used in the crime and his fingerprints all over everything, but Jules continues to cry from the rooftop that he didn't kill your uncle. No confession, and through all this, that brainless brute, Lejeune, keeps writing about us in his rag like we're stupid."

"If you are so convinced that Talbot is your man, how come you look so down in the dumps?" Catherine ventured.

The police officer scratched his head.

"Well, now, I've got to tell you: this whole case is turning pretty weird. We haven't just found Talbot's prints on the knife handle. There were others."

"What difference does that make? It's a butcher knife. It would be normal for one of his employees to use it in the days leading up to the murder, wouldn't it?"

Catherine could detect a grimace on the policeman's face.

"Not so sure," the policeman replied, thinking out loud. "Let's put ourselves in the guilty man's shoes. You see, unless it's a crime of passion, a murder is rarely committed on an impulse. I've worked on criminal investigations long enough to know that. The whole deal is planned in advance, and, in theory, it's perfect. No glitches. The murderer takes the time to study the comings and goings of his victim for a while, chooses the opportune moment to strike, and boom! Action! If Jules really used this knife, I'd wager my next meal that he wouldn't have let it hang around in the butcher shop in plain sight for days before the murder. It would have been too risky for him. An employee could have said he saw it or even used it. No, in my opinion, Jules cleaned the knife several days before, sharpened it, and made sure it was put away until he planned to use it. And what's more, it sliced like a guillotine during the French Revolution on the night of the murder."

"So what's your theory?"

"I don't have a theory. Just speculations. And a lot of things are still bothering me about Talbot. First, how would he have known that your Uncle J.A. would be at the cemetery around eleven o'clock the night of the murder? Those two haven't spoken to each other for years! And then there's that flower that J.A. was holding tight in his hand at the time of his death, as though his life depended on it. Someone must have wanted to give us a clue, but what does it mean?"

Roméo Dubuc stood up and filled their cups again.

"Is it possible that Talbot isn't your murderer?" Catherine asked, rather surprised by this idea.

"That's the question that keeps bugging me. Is it possible that Talbot isn't the murderer, or isn't the only murderer?"

Catherine slid Marie-Ève over to the chair next to her so she could give the police officer her full attention.

"You think he might have had an accomplice, because of all the prints on the knife?"

Dubuc's only reply was to take out the pendant with the little black cat and place it on the table.

"Don't forget this, Catherine. It's not the kind of a jewellery an honest parishioner would have misplaced when he went to say his pious prayers at the tomb of his dear mother. It's a fetish, a special object that belongs to members of that cult. I found one in the pocket of my son André the night of his death and you brought back another one from the cemetery the other day, right near the spot where your Uncle J.A. was said to have been brutally murdered. You draw your own conclusions."

The policeman sat down again, stretched out his legs and crossed his hands behind his neck.

"You think Talbot might have been part of the cult?" Catherine ventured.

Dubuc seemed to agree.

"That's where I'm at for the moment. But did he act alone? With an accomplice? I can't say. And I'm starting to believe more and more firmly that he committed the murder in the name of the cult."

"Did you think my uncle belonged to the cult too?" asked an anxious Catherine.

"Hard to say. I haven't got all the elements in hand in order to conclude that two and two make four. In an out-of-the-way place like Chesterville, we don't have a lot of resources. I'm overloaded. On the other hand, I've always thought that what mattered to your uncle was money and sex. But maybe I'm wrong."

Catherine drained her cup at one go and turned towards Marie-Ève.

"Anyway, I'd better get going. Poor Barbara must be thinking we'll never get back to the campground."

After Catherine left the Police Station, Chief Dubuc slipped into Lucien's office.

"Follow them at a distance, would you? And make darn sure they don't notice you."

★

Back in his office, the second line had already been flashing for some time. He picked up the receiver. It was Jeannot Lejeune. The police officer raised his eyes skyward: bad things always happened in threes.

"I don't have all day, Lejeune. On a scale of one to ten, my impatience is already up around twenty-two!"

"Don't take it out on me! You know what they say: don't kill the messenger! I'm just doing my job as a reporter," whined Lejeune on the other end of the line.

"Doing what? That's what I'd like to know! Writing for rags like the *Clarion* ? You should have stayed with vacuum cleaners, Johnny boy. You would have been of more use to society than you are with that paper that isn't fit to wipe my bum with!"

"You weren't quite so hard on me when I put your picture on the front page of my 'rag' as you call it, with a thirty-two inch long northern pike on the end of your fishing rod. It seems to me that one good turn deserves another. It's payback time."

"If you want me to pay you back for something, you'll have to put it on my tab for today."

"Seriously, Chief, just one question. I found out that Talbot's prints weren't the only ones on the weapon used in the crime. True or false?"

The heavy silence, loaded with a bonus of frustration, seemed to confirm Lejeune's scoop. The latter giggled with satisfaction.

"Some days, Johnny boy, you amaze me. Who did you sleep with to get that tidbit?"

"Not with your wife, that's for sure!" replied Lejeune, tit for tat.

"Let me give you a friendly warning. If you publish that in your pigsty press, you're going to have to learn to type with a prosthesis. Is that clear?"

"Wake up, Chief! If my information is true, Talbot might not be the suspect you're looking for."

"Not so fast, Boy. Don't forget that Jules left his fingerprints all over the knife. That's enough to make him my number one suspect. As for the rest of it, well, I'm looking for an explanation. And I'll find it, you can be sure of that. *Adios!*"

He slammed down the receiver. The sensation of cutting off the reporter calmed him for a fraction of a second, but then his worries came back even more urgently. What if Lejeune was right?

The telephone rang again. It was Stan Rubinsky.

"I have bad news," the psychiatrist said, in a voice that was barely audible. "It's about Conrad. We just found him, behind the hospital. He hanged himself."

⋆

Roméo Dubuc called Lucien back in. It was urgent. They rushed over to the Chesterville Psychiatric Hospital.

"Shoot and double-shoot!" repeated Dubuc, all the way to the scene of the crime, while the police siren screeched.

They were soon under the imposing shadow of the hospital. They drove along the west side of the austere building to save some time, but they were quickly confronted with a high fence that had recently been built around the back of the hospital. They had no choice but to turn around and go back, then run to the main entrance and cross the entire length of the hospital.

When they finally got to the back of the hospital, the police officer took a deep breath. Here, the decor was far from austere. They were in a large, lush green park where tulips, roses and other bushes elegantly lined the walkways and paths that led to a little farm situated at about two hundred metres behind the hospital. In normal circumstances, thirty patients or so were occupied with gardening and landscaping, with the dairy herd and in the chicken coop, ensuring the production of food for the kitchens of the institution. For certain patients, this activity was a stepping stone between the hospital and their return to a more normal life outside.

When he reached the barn, Chief Dubuc and Lucien found terrified staff members and patients huddled together. They cleared a path for themselves through the crowd and went up to the front. All eyes were glued on the loft, where the tragedy had occurred. When the policemen raised their eyes in the same direction, they grasped the full extent of the drama: Conrad Bussières's inert body dangled from the end of a thick hemp rope, knotted and tied to a beam of the barn's loft, about five metres above their heads. The expression of terror on the victim's face left no doubt about the suffering he had gone through before giving up the ghost.

"Here you are at last!" raged Stan Rubinsky, leading them by the arm to the scene of the drama. "What a tragedy! Follow me up to the loft!"

One by one, they climbed up the roughly-made ladder that went up to the loft, where hay and farming tools were stored haphazardly. Chief Dubuc opened the little door of the loft and saw Conrad's body hanging a few metres below.

"I imagine that the hay is usually passed up through this door so it can be stored in the loft, is that it?"

Dr. Rubinsky's only reply was to turn to a solidly-built man of about thirty, who sniffed noisily nearby.

"This is Serge Brindle, our farm manager. He supervises the employees. He's the one who discovered the body and he'll be able to answer your questions.

Dubuc beckoned him over.

"Where were you when . . . "

"Over there, on the tractor," replied Brindle, rubbing his hands together nervously. "I was coming to check how the hay cutting was going when I saw him hanging there in space like a bag of potatoes."

"Still alive?"

"Not as far as I know. He was dangling there from the rope, you understand."

"I see. And then?"

"Nothing."

"What do you mean, nothing?" Dubuc asked, astonished. "And will you please stop rubbing your hands like that? You're making everyone nervous."

"I'm not used to the police," retorted the other, putting his hands into his pockets. "When I saw the body, I ran to the hospital to tell Dr. Rubinsky."

"Well, well! And why him in particular?"

The psychiatrist interrupted them.

"Serge knew that Conrad was under the influence of powerful medication and . . . "

Dubuc interrupted.

"Let me finish questioning your farm manager."

He motioned to Brindle to continue.

"Dr. Rubinsky had told me to let him know if anything ever happened to Conrad.

"And had anything happened before?"

Serge Brindle lowered his eyes, but Dubuc had the distinct impression that he was shooting a sideways glance in the doctor's direction.

"Had it happened before?" repeated the policeman.

"Not really serious stuff. The first time, Conrad threw a fit with a patient. He was screaming like a madman!"

"Another fight," sighed the doctor.

"I got there just in time to separate them," said Brindle. "The next time was when Conrad fell into a manure heap."

"He could have died in there!"

"That's true," replied Brindle. "But I had two employees who screamed so loud we got him out of there real fast."

Dr. Rubinsky turned towards Dubuc.

"We interpreted Conrad's gesture as a suicide attempt that failed, that time."

"You think so?"

"It's obvious. My colleagues and I have been observing Conrad long enough in the clinic to know. The poor boy suffered from a horrible inferiority complex when his father was around, and harboured very dark thoughts towards him. His father had succeeded in life, and made Conrad feel that he was good for nothing, a loser. I'm not saying that it was Conrad who killed his father, but I am prepared to state that he had reached the mental state necessary to commit such an act. Draw your own conclusions. Obviously, J.A.'s death changed his plans, and all Conrad's violence that had been directed towards his father. He turned it all towards himself and committed suicide."

The psychiatrist bobbed his head in a self-satisfied manner.

"Amazing," repeated Dubuc, rather dazzled by this exposé.

"Anyway, it's a frequent motive for suicide," continued

Rubinsky. "When one becomes unable to direct one's violence towards others, one turns it against oneself. We have at least one case like that every year at the hospital. We try to keep it as quiet as possible, as you can imagine. The pressure on certain patients becomes so strong that they crack."

The doctor went over and stood by the door through which Conrad had jumped towards his death.

"I'll help you pull the body back up and you'll see that . . . "

Roméo Dubuc came forward and pulled roughly on his arm.

"No one touches Conrad until the coroner gets here."

A few minutes later, the old doctor arrived and had a ladder installed to reach the body, still hanging in the air. Dubuc was anxious about the whole operation, given the advanced age of the coroner.

"Are you sure you're all right, Dr. Moreau?" he shouted up.

The coroner just waved his hand as he continued to climb up the ladder leaning against the wall of the barn. Despite the horror of the drama, there was a touch of black humour in the sight of the old man. Perched on the ladder, he was risking his own neck trying to stop Conrad's body from moving. It continued to dangle from the noose. The coroner carried out a preliminary examination in about fifteen minutes, and then climbed back down.

"It's all right!" he shouted to the group in the loft. "You can cut him down. I'm finished for the moment."

He almost fell down the ladder when Marguerita Bussières made her appearance, grabbing the attention of the crowd.

Dubuc turned to the psychiatrist. "Find some sort of reason to keep her here for another five minutes. I have to take care of an urgent matter. Quick, Lucien, help me pull the body back up."

"I'm not surprised," said the deputy, straining under the effort of dragging the body up onto the floor of the loft.

"About what?"

"That Conrad decided to end it all."

Roméo Dubuc wasn't listening any more. He was leaning over Conrad's lifeless body and he noticed several yellowish stains along the rope, similar to those that had been found on the handle of the butcher knife used to kill J.A.

He put his hand on Conrad's cheek. The skin was still warm to the touch. The flow of blood provoked by the hanging had, however, given the face and the neck a repulsive, purplish hue.

"The time of death was at most an hour ago," said Chief Dubuc. "Which means that Conrad was still alive at four o'clock this afternoon."

He dug his thumb into the victim's skin in several different spots. Conrad's complexion, as well as a quick observation of his lips and nails, confirmed the police chief's impressions.

"I'm going to try to find some patients who might have talked to Conrad before four o'clock," said Lucien, heading down the stairs.

"And try to find out whether he really gave the impression that he was depressed, as his act would suggest."

The policeman remained there a moment, looking pensively at the body. The arrival of the ambulance cut his lethargy short. He went straight to the Police Station, closed the door of his office and served himself a glass of gin. A double.

Chapter 10

A ringing telephone pulled Roméo Dubuc out of his alcohol-induced fog. Gilberte had woken up and realized that her husband hadn't come home that night.

"You know very well that I'm not in the habit of staying out all night! I fell asleep at work last night. That's all! I needed a second body about as much as I needed a bullet in the head. I'll call you back when I'm on my lunch."

The police officer got up with some difficulty. He washed up quickly and poured himself a coffee. Lucien came in the door at that point; Catherine followed close behind him.

"Looking at those puffy eyes, I'd say you heard the news," he commented.

"I just can't believe it!" exclaimed Catherine. "When I was young, Conrad was a bit like the little brother I never had. Later he got sick, and that kept us apart, but still . . . "

"How is your aunt doing?"

"My guess is that Marguerita won't stick around here. She had signed a prenuptial agreement with my uncle. As long as Conrad was alive, she had to look after his material needs whenever he wasn't in the hospital. But now that he's gone, I don't think she'll hang around much longer in Chesterville. She's always hated living here anyway."

"I hadn't even thought of what Conrad's death would mean for Marguerita," the policeman admitted. "On the other hand, I know that J.A.'s fortune went in equal parts to your aunt and Conrad. Almost two million dollars. Hardly what you'd call peanuts!"

"My uncle also made sure that if either of the two heirs died, his entire fortune would go to the one who was left."

The police officer giggled with satisfaction.

"Marguerita's going to get the whole jackpot. Four million dollars!"

"I hope I'm not getting my aunt into hot water," Catherine said with a worried look on her face.

"Not at all. Marguerita was already up to her neck in boiling water as it was."

The telephone rang again. It was the coroner calling to say he was on his way. Dubuc thought he detected a bit of excitement in his voice. Catherine crossed paths with the old doctor as she left the police station.

Dubuc obviously had a lot of respect for Dr. Moreau, the coroner. The little man was from what was called "the old school." With his symphony-conductor style and his eternal bow tie, he could carry out his autopsies like a meister, and with the patience of a Benedictine monk, persisting over a minute detail when it was necessary. Over his forty-year career, he had accumulated an impressive toolbag of medical expertise. That's why Dubuc was astonished to see him arrive with such a spark in his eyes.

When the police officer commented on it, Ernest Moreau didn't hide his interest in this particular case.

"You have a passion for these suicide cases?" asked Dubuc in a detached tone of voice.

"Suicides? Please, let's be serious! It's a murder, Roméo. Conrad Bussières was killed. The autopsy was done in Montréal and the results are still preliminary, but I know enough about it to know you'll be losing a month's worth of sleep over this one."

The police chief slumped down into the chair, as though he were about to collapse. This was the moment the coroner was waiting for. He pulled out a large sketch pad from his bag, took out a marker and outlined the silhouette of a human head.

"When we are in the company of a hanged man, how do we distinguish the victim of suicide from that of a murder?" he asked in a pedantic tone, his eye still gleaming.

"I've never thought about it!" Dubuc exclaimed. "And yet in thirty years on the job I've certainly seen a few deaths by hanging. But when someone is dangling from the end of a rope, maybe it's just me, but I always assume it's a suicide."

The coroner giggled with satisfaction, as though the demonstration he was about to begin was simply a formality.

"I don't blame you," he continued. "Murders by hanging are very rare in the annals of North American police records. I would even say that, unless you were really looking for certain, precise signs of a murder, anyone would probably miss them and conclude it was a suicide."

"What makes you suspect a homicide in this case?" asked Dubuc, his interest piqued.

"The door of the hayloft. The one through which they would have us believe the victim fell to his death. Did you notice?" asked the coroner, sketching something on his pad.

"Not really."

"When I asked you to bring the body up, I noticed that the door was rather wide but low, which is quite unusual for a hayloft door. I know because I grew up on a farm. To manage to hang himself, Conrad would have had to be able to leap into the void with considerable momentum. But that door is too low for that to be possible. He couldn't really have jumped down below without banging his head. At the very most, he could have let himself slide and strangle himself slowly at the end of the rope. I believe you'll agree with me that it's highly unlikely that this poor lad would have hanged himself this way. Which brings me to my suspicion that he was probably already dead when he was propelled into the void at the end of his rope."

"Did your autopsy show that to be the case?"

"When it's finished, it will certainly show that. But I know enough to keep you interested. You see, Roméo, with a hanging, it's really the shape of the abrasion left by the rope around the neck that allows us to determine if we are dealing with a suicide or a murder. Look: if a fellow hangs himself, the rope always leaves a mark like an upside-down 'V' around the neck, like this one, caused by the weight of the body projected to the ground. Are you still with me?"

"Pretty much. And in the case of a murder?"

"This is where the story gets interesting for you. Here, as you may have noticed, if you looked at the body the upside-down 'V' was very obvious on Conrad's neck."

"It was horrible to look at," confirmed Dubuc. "I had to get myself out of there. The poor kid had a face as purple as a beet."

"I understand. But if you had stay to examine Conrad's neck more thoroughly, you may have noticed that, right near that mark, there was another one. It wasn't as deep as that one, and formed a horizontal scar on the skin: the typical mark left by a thin wire."

"Two marks?" Dubuc was astonished.

"Yes, two. And what confirms my suspicions is this: the bruises left on the nape of his neck. Conrad's murderer certainly pushed down with his hand quite forcefully on the victim's neck to strangle him first, rolling a steel wire around his neck. This's what left the bluish marks."

"A murder," Dubuc murdered.

"That is probably what happened, Roméo. A murder disguised as a suicide. When he was being strangled, Conrad must have fought back until he suffocated. Given the fact he was taking rather strong anti-psychotic medication, he probably didn't fight for long. Afterwards, his murderer had only to push him into the void at the end of his rope, and Conrad broke his neck on the way down, making it look like a suicide."

For a moment, Dubuc was speechless, stupefied by the turn the events had taken.

"I knew you would be astonished by what I had to say," Dr. Moreau said, satisfied with his demonstration.

"You can say that again!"

"I'll leave you to your work then. I have several more tests to do that will end up taking all night."

⋆

The coroner's prediction was right: Roméo Dubuc was unable to sleep that night. He was turning J.A. Bussières's murder, and now that of his son Conrad, over and over in his head. He kept asking himself the same questions. Why two murders? Was it the same killer in both cases? What did the Cult of the Cat have to do with all this? Dubuc reflected long and hard before finally falling asleep in the wee hours of the morning. But his sleep was haunted by little devilish creatures with forked tails dancing around J.A. and his son. He woke up in a cold sweat. His alarm clock read six-eighteen a.m. He got up, gulped down a coffee and a big breakfast and then went to his office. To his surprise, Lucien was already at work, even though it was a Saturday morning.

"I passed Doc Moreau last night, coming out. I knew you'd be on the trail early in the morning. It's pretty easy to figure out you didn't get any sleep last night."

"And not much all week," complained the officer. "I still don't know why J.A. was murdered, and now here I am with his son's body on my hands too."

"Do you think Talbot might be involved in both murders?" asked Lucien, although he could guess what the answer would be.

"Let's be serious for a moment. Talbot is in the slammer. Has been since Wednesday night. That gives us one less suspect in Conrad's death."

"Have you got any evidence that the two murders are connected?!

"Not yet. But I don't think it'll take long before I do. Maybe the autopsy will tell us more about the *modus operandi* of the murder. I'm counting on Dr. Moreau to shed some light on it. I'm on my way to the hospital now to open up my investigation, but something tells me that it's going to be a waste of time."

★

"I've been hiding something from you," Stan Rubinsky announced as the police chief walked into his office.

"It's getting to be a habit!" Dubuc was astonished. "And what is it this time?"

The doctor closed the door behind him and sat down on the corner of his desk, looking quite awkward.

"Don't be rude! It isn't deliberate. It's about our farm manager, Serge Brindle. You met him. It's a bit delicate. Serge has a record. I didn't know it when I hired him but I thought I'd better tell you myself, before you heard it from someone else."

"Was it for a serious offence?"

"I'm afraid so. In the circumstances. Serge did three years in prison for stabbing someone he worked with. It was about ten years ago. The man's been an invalid ever since."

"Had he already been involved in this kind of thing at work?"

"Not that I know of. But one of the nurses in my

department used to go out with him. Apparently Serge can be hard to predict."

"Interesting. Can you bring him to me?"

Ten minutes later, Chief Dubuc found himself with Brindle in a little room identical to the one where he had questioned Conrad a few days earlier. The witness was sitting down with his hands on the table in front of him. Dubuc stood in a corner of the room, his arms folded. A few metres away from each other, they watched each other like two wild animals. Only the four eyes were moving, furtively, around the still room.

Serge Brindle was squat but sturdy. Dubuc paid particularly close attention to his hands, which were short, solid and calloused. They were the hands of a labourer, and maybe of a strangler, as well. What attracted the attention of the police officer was the intensity of Brindle's gaze. It kept Dubuc on high alert. Was it provocation? Resistance? Hesitation? Or maybe it was just awkwardness. He was about to find out.

"Are you going to keep me long?" Brindle asked suddenly.

"I'm the one asking the questions here, Serge."

"It's just that I have my work to . . . "

"That's enough!" bellowed Dubuc, making Brindle jump. "Your job is to answer my questions. Get it?"

The other nodded. Dubuc could see out of the corner of his eye that he had won a point. Brindle had his tail between his legs.

"Is that the first body you've found?" he continued.

"Yes, the first."

"Do you own any firearms?"

"No."

"I heard you were involved in another incident. A serious one, with a knife, right?"

"That was a long time ago. I was with another guy, a friend of mine, out drinking and it turned out badly. I stabbed him in the back with a pocketknife and he ended up partially paralyzed."

Brindle abruptly stopped talking. He bit his lips and began again, in a halting voice. "The guy is going to remain paralyzed for the rest of his life. When I see him in the park, in his wheelchair, with his little girl – it breaks my heart. I wish I could change places with him."

"You mean . . . "

"Some days, I don't have the will to live. It's simple. I just want to put an end to it all."

Unexpectedly, the policeman went up to Serge Brindle and put his revolver on the table in front of him. He pointed at the special .38.

"Go ahead. Take it."

Brindle looked at him, confused.

"I said, take my revolver."

"Why?"

"Take it!"

"No. No way."

Roméo Dubuc picked up his gun and left the room.

*

The police officer headed for the barn where Conrad's body had been found. At the farm behind the hospital, people were back to their normal routines. Dubuc wanted to see the scene of the crime again, now that the coroner had dismissed the suicide hypothesis.

His arrival set a flock of pigeons into flight; they circled around above his head in the barn as he climbed awkwardly up the ladder. He was out of breath by the time he got up to the loft. Squatting next to the spot where Conrad's body had been hoisted up, he started thinking out loud.

"Let's see. If Conrad had been fighting back when the murderer attacked, he must have been right about here."

He stood up and walked a few metres over to where the plank was hanging above his head.

"For him to be able to get the rope around his neck, the killer must have been standing right near the beam, here."

Roméo Dubuc turned again, this time towards the back of the hayloft, with his eyes still riveted to the ground. Suddenly, what he saw a few centimetres from his left foot sent a shiver up his spine: daisy petals. The same wildflower that had been found in the clenched fist of Bussières's body in the cemetery. He leaned over, picked it up delicately and placed it in the palm of his hand. His gaze remained frozen and his heart was pounding.

He immediately returned to the police station, both satisfied and worried. Satisfied, because he was now convinced that the murders of Bussières and Conrad were committed by the same person. Worried, because he knew this discovery was leading him closer to the terrifying Cult of the Cat.

Lucien Langlois did not entirely agree with his deductions.

"Flower petals deliberately left at the scene? What kind of murderer would be stupid enough to leave such obvious clues behind?"

"No ordinary murderer, of course. But in all likelihood, J.A. and Conrad were both killed by the same person. The daisies found in J.A.'s hand and left near Conrad's body are the only clue we have to link these two ritual murders. In my opinion, they're the calling card that the cult leaves."

"You really think the cult would dabble in murder?"

Dubuc had obviously considered the question.

"In my experience, murderers are usually a bit lazy. They lack imagination. If what they do works once, they'll use the same method a second time. It's the law of the least effort. But with J.A. and Conrad, the cases proceeded in a very different way. J.A. was murdered during the night and Conrad in broad daylight. J.A. was stabbed but Conrad was hanged. J.A. died in a remote area and Conrad in a farm where thirty people worked. Why would an ordinary killer take so many risks changing the scene of the crime? Which leads me to believe that the Cult of the Cat must be directly involved. I think it's acting this way to capture our imagination. And also to hide its tracks."

Catherine Gagnon arrived in the midst of his speech. She was taken aback, and stood there for a moment watching Chief Dubuc and Lucien sigh helplessly over some flower petals on the table in front of them.

Dubuc summarized the latest discoveries quickly for her.

"So you think it's important, this wild daisy?" Catherine asked.

"It's sort of our 'missing link.' The thing that makes us believe that J.A.'s murder and Conrad's were planned and committed by the Cult of the Cat. But who, how and why, I really have no idea."

Catherine shared his sentiment.

"I can recall a number of American sociological studies that show that people who appear to be well-balanced and who lead an ordinary life can belong to organizations or cults that are quite dangerous. Like the Cult of the Cat. It's almost as though they lead a double life."

"Anyone in Chesterville could belong, you mean?"

"Even people very close to you," added Catherine.

She carefully picked up the delicate daisy petals and placed them in the palm of her hand, as though the flower had magical powers to conjure up the cult's shady presence in Chesterville.

"It's funny," she said, after a moment. "Jerry Ménard also wears a daisy as a boutonnière. I noticed it the first time when we were at the Greluche, and then again on Thursday when he made me get into his car with him."

Dubuc jumped up.

"Jerry, you're right! Now that I think about it, I noticed it too the other night at the club when I was questioning him."

"It's part of his Perfect Seducer kit," Catherine said. She burst out laughing. "That, and his cheap aftershave and those toady eyes. Oh, he's just soooo irresistible!"

"The most amazing thing," Dubuc said, trying to keep his excitement under control, "is that Ménard claims he's allergic to flowers. At the funeral home, he kept sneezing and wiping his nose."

"Maybe so, but the vase on his desk was full of wild daisies, that night we were together at the Greluche. Swear to God, I'm sure of it," continued Catherine emphatically.

"Hold on a minute. If what you're saying is right, Ménard's going to have some serious explaining to do!"

"And don't forget he's always hanging around in the bushes when his ex-wives are killed," remarked Lucien. "Those old stories never really got cleared up. I tend to believe that our friend Jerry is a master in the art of disguising murders as suicides."

*

Catherine put Marie-Ève to bed and went to join Barbara, who was sitting next to the fire. It was almost nine o'clock in the evening. The area around the campground was quite noisy on this summer Saturday night. All over the campground, there were other fires being lit. Suddenly they heard screams from inside the tent and rushed inside. Marie-Ève was sitting on her camp cot, shaking in terror. Catherine woke her up from her nightmare.

"I saw ghosts, Mama! Ghosts who were killing little babies with a knife!"

Catherine sat on the edge of her cot and comforted her by pulling her into her arms.

"Darling, you know very well there's no such thing as ghosts. It was just a bad dream."

"It was not!" retorted Marie-Ève, wide awake now. "Sophie saw ghosts who killed baby kittens with knives in the woods!"

"Sophie is at home asleep like a good little girl. And you should go to sleep now too, Marie-Ève," Catherine said sternly.

The little girl was, however, a long way from being ready to go to sleep. She was beyond herself. "They made Sophie hurt the kittens, Mama!"

Catherine took her daughter by the shoulders and looked her in the eye. Marie-Ève was wide awake and was telling horrific tales in her child's words. Catherine stayed beside her for quite a while, until she could feel the breathing of her daughter who was huddled against her become heavy once again.

★

With his eagle eye and the patience of an angel, Roméo studied his prey throughout the entire weekend. He spied on Jerry Ménard, watching every move he made and planning his interrogation. But he was not about to do this wherever and however it just happened. Dubuc had noticed a shadowy figure, an unshaven individual, discreetly following the club-owner around. One of his hired apes, probably. There was no doubt about it: Jerry could tell he was in a stew. The policeman had his little ideas about what was going on. He was waiting for the right moment.

It came on Monday night, at around nine o'clock. Ménard had stopped at the Esso station on the outskirts of Chesterville. The police officer checked and confirmed that he was, indeed, by himself.

Jerry Ménard motioned to the gas station attendant to fill up his car. Meanwhile, he went into the washrooms behind the garage. Dubuc chose this exact moment to intervene. Ménard hadn't even unzipped his fly before he felt a less-than-friendly hand push his shoulders up against the wall, while the officer slammed the door shut in the minuscule room. Acting on a reflex, Jerry immediately slid his left hand into the pocket of his jacket, but let go of his gun when he felt the barrel of a .38 pressed to his temple.

"Easy, Jerry. If you're not careful, an accident might happen. Let go of your little toy pistol. That's better. You know I could book you for carrying an illegal weapon?"

"You haven't got anything on me!" Ménard said, with a nervous look.

"I need to talk to you in private, Ménard, but you always have your apes hanging around. You'd think you were the prime minister!"

"Hey, I've got a good lawyer!"

"I'm just dying to meet him," responded Dubuc, suddenly pulling the daisy out of Ménard's boutonnière. "My, my . . . and I thought you were allergic to flowers!"

"Except daisies. It's the only one I can stand without having a runny nose for two days afterwards. But I have trouble believing you followed me into the can just to discuss botany with me."

"Calm down now, Jerry. You see, that darned flower has

been giving me nightmares. I found one in the fist of J.A.'s corpse and then, again, right near his son's body. You gotta admit, it's a pretty odd coincidence. How come it shows up every time at the scene of the crime? I thought that maybe you'd be able to help me figure that out."

Jerry Ménard switched his tone of voice and adopted a more cooperative attitude that raised the chief's suspicions.

"You know that I'd help you if I could. It's just that what you're saying is all Greek to me. What makes you think I know anything about it?"

"Your activities on the night of J.A.'s murder, rat-face! That's what! With all your comings and goings, your alibi is about as leaky as a basket of water. I've already chatted with five or six clients leering at your dancers at the Greluche, between ten p.m. and closing time that night. No one remembers seeing you at the club, Jerry. Not a one."

There was a grimace on Jerry's face for a fraction of a second before his survival instinct won out.

"That's what it's like. Some nights I'm there, I don't see a soul. I park in the back of the club and I go straight to my office."

"Nevertheless, Jerry . . . "

The police officer took out his notebook and leafed through it. "At the funeral home the other night, you claimed that you had a 'ton of witnesses' to confirm your comings and goings at Greluche the night of J.A.'s murder. I've got it written down right here. Are you changing your story? Are you saying now that only Carabosse the wicked witch knew you were at the Greluche the night of the murder?"

The policeman placed his notebook on side of the sink, let Ménard take a breath, and folded his arms across his chest. The disgusting smell of urine that floated in the air twisted his nostrils, but he managed to keep it under control. Standing less than a metre in front of him, Jerry Ménard didn't know where to look. He swivelled around like a leech and looked nervously around the tiny room, as though the answer might fall from the heavens.

The policeman grabbed hold of the lining of his jacket and put the daisy he had removed a few moments before back in place. Finally, he opened the door behind him.

"I have a feeling I'm getting really warm, Jerry. You'd better be telling the truth, or else watch your balls, you little dickens."

Chapter 11

When Roméo Dubuc got back to the police station later that evening, Dr. Moreau was waiting in his car. He headed straight towards him.

The policeman took note of the old coroner's suggestive smile. He could guess that there was some new development he wanted to share. Dubuc sat down on the front seat of the car. Ernest Moreau wasted no time getting to the point.

"The autopsy showed that Conrad Bussières was taking quite a cocktail of powerful medications. According to our tests, his psychiatrist had prescribed two anti-psychotics that were strong enough to put a horse out of commission."

"What's this story you're telling me?" retorted Dubuc.

"The truth, Roméo. I would prefer not to criticize the decision of a medical colleague, but it was important that you know. Taken one at a time, either of these medications usually has beneficial results for schizophrenic patients. But when given together, they are like lit sticks of dynamite."

Ernest Moreau picked up a pile of papers from the back seat of the car.

"I found a few medical studies that suggest the fact that, taken together, the two drugs can increase the neurological toxicity of the patient. Patients might experience confusion, dizziness, and trembling. When I said that Conrad was probably unable to fight against his assailant, I was correct. He must have been completely out of it by the time he was attacked.

"Was this type of treatment justified in your opinion?"

The coroner shrugged his shoulders. "It's hard to say. I'm not a psychiatrist and I wouldn't want to take a position on it. But what might be of interest to you in your investigation is that Stan Rubinsky had been administering this combination of medications for only a few days before the crime."

The police officer opened his notebook and carefully recorded the information. "A few days, you say? Very interesting."

*

Stan Rubinsky had barely finished his second appointment before Dubuc arrived, unannounced, in his office.

"I need to talk to you. Immediately," the police officer stated firmly.

The psychiatrist could tell the policeman hadn't slept by his puffy face. He sat down behind his desk and invited Dubuc to do the same.

"You're working too hard, Chief. Look at you! If you continue this way, you'll soon be suffering from burnout."

The Siberian look prompted him to change the subject.

"How long have you been treating Conrad?"

"I don't know. Five or six years, I guess."

"During that period, did his condition improve at all?"

"Well, yes and no. By the end, Conrad was not responding well to his medication plan."

"Were the drugs you gave him useful, would you say?"

"For schizophrenia, they were. You know, psychotherapy sessions really don't have much of an effect on this type of illness, unfortunately."

"What did you prescribe for him?"

The psychiatrist stood up, put both hands in the pocket of his white lab coat and approached the policeman.

"No offense, but I need to respect professional confidentiality. Conrad was my patient and I . . . "

Dubuc leapt to his feet and bound over to the psychiatrist, posting himself under his nose. "I'm investigating the death of one of your patients and you're talking about doctor-patient confidentiality? Let me tell you something, Dr. Rubinsky. Conrad did not commit suicide. He was murdered. The autopsy report shows that you changed Conrad's medication a few days before his death. You gave him a combination of two very powerful anti-psychotics, both at heavy doses. As a result, he was incapable of defending himself when he was attacked in the hayloft."

Roméo Dubuc could barely contain himself. An orderly who had heard his outcry from the hall came into the office.

"Problems, Dr. Rubinsky?"

The psychiatrist reassured him and sent him on his way. He tried to calm the police officer and get him to sit down again.

"I know how overworked you are these days. Gosh, another murder. I imagine this investigation is starting to take its toll on your health. You're not looking too good, right now. Here, have something to drink."

He held out a glass of cold water and sat down next to the officer.

"Contrary to what you might believe, psychiatric medicine is not an exact science. If we give someone a pill, we're never sure whether it will have the desired benefits. The same is true with harmful effects. Medications are unpredictable. Some patients respond to the treatments, and others don't do as well. I'm looking at a recent approach that consists of scientifically combining the two best-known anti-psychotics in order to produce more effective clinical results. It's the most frequent approach used these days in the United States. It's hoped that, by combining them, it will be possible to decrease the trembling you noticed in

Conrad. But in order to find out if it would work, we had to give it a try. That's what I did."

"Just a few days before Conrad's death. You have to admit, it's an odd coincidence."

"I agree. Chance seems to have played out in a strange way, but that's what happened. When you brought Conrad back after his escape, I did my best to modify his treatment so that his condition would improve. I admit that I took risks, but I was aware of them. With schizophrenia, Chief Dubuc, even apparently insignificant progress is useful. Who knows? Conrad might have been finally getting out of his private hell and onto the road to recovery. Sadly, we'll never find out."

The police officer had got over his strong emotions and left Dr. Rubinsky's office. But the dark expression on his face suggested he was unconvinced.

★

When he arrived at the station, Chief Dubuc saw that Catherine was engaged in a discussion with Lucien. He passed between the two of them without saying hello, and then closed himself into his office, leaving them intrigued by his brief appearance.

"Brrr. It's going to be a long day," sighed Lucien. "When the boss gets that look on his face, it's a bad sign of what's to come."

Catherine tentatively walked to the door and knocked softly. When she went in, she was astonished to see the policeman's face covered in shaving cream and a razor in his hand.

"I'm worried," she began.

"Mmmmm. Worried about what?" he asked, as he continued shaving with quick, dry strokes.

"I was just telling Lucien that Marie-Ève had a nightmare last night. When I woke her up, she started telling me horrible things about Sophie."

"What things?"

"Marie-Ève said that Sophie had taken part in murders of animals in the woods. Kittens. It's disturbing, don't you think?"

"You know as well as I do that Marie-Ève is very sensitive, and Sophie-in-Wonderland Ménard has more imagination than she knows what to do with. I certainly got proof of that the other day. She's probably invented the drama for your daughter's benefit."

"No, you don't understand!" exclaimed Catherine. "Marie-Ève was wide awake, completely conscious when she told me those things about Sophie. She wasn't dreaming, or making it up."

Dubuc put down his razor with a distracted air. He plunged his face into a wet towel and turned towards Catherine.

"Is Sophie still in the hospital?"

"No, the doctors had her undergo a psychiatric exam and gave her some tests. They're still waiting for the results. She was discharged the day after she was admitted. Apparently Jerry had a hissy fit when they told him her daughter was suffering from malnutrition. He started screeching about her being normal and everything. Sophie is playing with Marie-Ève and Barbara at the campground.

"Come on, let's go. I want to talk to her."

*

Barbara Watkins was leaning up against a tree, her eyes closed, and had nearly finished counting up to fifty.

"Forty-seven, forty-eight . . . "

Marie-Ève and Sophie were hiding behind a big stump about a hundred metres away from Barbara, holding their breath.

"It's not a very good hiding place," whispered Marie-Ève. "Barbara will find us right away."

"I know a much better place. Come with me!" Sophie said, leading her friend away by the hand.

They ran down the hillside to the pond beside Lac des Sables while Barbara went off looking for them, combing the bushes and wooded area around the tent.

"Where are you, Girls? Girls!"

Marie-Ève took Coconut in her arms. They made their way across the pond, stepping on big, flat rocks. Now they were headed through the field on the other side of the pond, directly across from the campground. Fifteen minutes later, Marie-Ève turned around, her face suddenly overcome with worry. She hugged Coconut. "We've gone far enough, Sophie! Barbara will never find us here. We have to go back to the campground. My mother's going to get worried."

"You're with me!" Sophie said. "Are you scared?"

"No," Marie-Ève replied, hesitantly.

"If you come with me into the woods, I'll show you something."

"What? What?" cried Marie-Ève, jumping up and down with excitement.

"It's a secret."

Marie-Ève's eyes were sparkling with curiosity. "A secret?"

"Yeah. It's the place where the ghosts kill little kitties."

Marie-Ève took Sophie's hand again, and was led into the forest.

*

Dubuc was on his way out to join Catherine in the patrol car when he dropped his keys. Leaning over to pick them up, a pair of scarlet slippers suddenly came into his line of vision. Still bending down, Dubuc burst out into uncontrollable laughter.

"Cripes! I only know one joker in Chesterville who is laid-back enough to go to work in red slippers. Must be Lejeune. We're in a hurry, my boy, so let's run like the wind!"

"It's good to see you, Chief. If I had to count on the police to keep my newspaper going I would have gone bankrupt years ago."

His comment made Dubuc freeze on the spot. He knew Lejeune well enough to know that if the reporter was tooting his horn that loudly it was because he had found out something new about the investigation. Worried, he got up and took Lejeune aside.

"I don't know what you've got in your ugly little head, Lejeune, but when you act like a bastard, I can't help but worry. Have you got a scoop or something?"

Dubuc had asked his question in a tone that betrayed his uncertainty. Lejeune was obviously enjoying it all, and took on an even more arrogant tone. He was going to have fun playing cat-and-mouse; that was clear.

"Now, let's just say there's a rumour going around."

"What rumour?"

"You know, all the finger-prints on Talbot's knife. You basically told me to go to hell when I asked about that the other day, remember?"

Dubuc clenched his fists angrily. He hated it when Lejeune pulled his strings like he was a puppet. But this time there was nothing he could do about it. He should have known. He put on a false air of contrition. "You're right. I'm sorry, Jeannot. You know me, I sometimes get too big for my britches. It's my nature."

"Yeah, that's what I figured. Anyway, all those fingerprints on the knife seem to suggest that the murders of J.A. Bussières and Conrad were ritualistic sacrifices, and were committed by members of a satanic cult. We can rule out the possibility they were crimes of passion, wouldn't you agree?"

The chief of police stood up, relieved, and feigned astonishment.

"Bravo! You've finally figured something out! And who told you this incredible piece of news? Don't tell me: your usual 'secret source,' right?" Dubuc was back to his old self now.

"Of course. But because I'm a good boy, I thought I should talk to you before."

"Before what?" asked Dubuc, nervous again.

"Before printing the photo, obviously."

Proud of himself, Jeannot Lejeune brandished an enlarged photo, as though he were a magician pulling a rabbit out of a hat. What Dubuc had before his eyes now confirmed his worse fears. The photo was dark, taken at night, and revealed a group of six or eight people dressed in long black robes and huddled around a tombstone in the cemetery. In the middle of the group, there was a little girl wearing a white wedding gown.

"Looks like a satanic ceremony," said Catherine, looking over the reporter's shoulder.

"Sure, but the photo's pretty fuzzy. It's impossible to identify the faces of this gang of sons-of-guns," retorted Dubuc.

He turned the photo around and looked at it from all angles. "That looks like Bussières's gravestone."

"It's Toto Grimaldi who took the photo, with his camera. Late last night."

"What the hell were they doing in the cemetery so late at night?" Dubuc exclaimed.

"From what I've heard, his wife had insisted that he finish up the greenhouse in his yard. It would've been almost midnight when he came to get his electric drill from the cemetery. That's when he heard some noise and went up to find out what was going on. Apparently he couldn't believe his eyes. He went back to his shed to get a little camera he keeps there. He uses it to take snapshots of the gravestones. I guess families ask for that a lot. Unfortunately, though, there wasn't enough light to make out any of the details."

"We'll have to talk to him right away," stated Dubuc.

"Don't waste your time," Lejeune cut in. "Toto has shut himself off in his house. Been there since last night. He's refusing to come out."

"His life is in danger, Jeannot."

Dubuc immediately got in touch with Lucien, and told him to put in a protection order. The Grimaldis' house would be guarded until further notice.

But his deputy had news that put Chief Dubuc's immediate plans on the back burner for a while. "Young Barbara Watkins just called. Marie-Ève and Sophie have disappeared."

*

The mid-afternoon sun filtered through the dense green forest, barely lighting showing through the leaves. Sophie darted through the trees, holding tightly onto Marie-Ève's hand. The little girl kept tripping as she made her way through the tangled path. Coconut followed a few metres behind them.

"Sophie, I'm tired! I want to stop."

"No way. We're almost there. Come on!"

They had been walking for almost an hour. Every once in a while, Sophie would stop and look around her, checking she was going the right way. Marie-Ève suddenly began to cry. "My feet hurt. I want to go home."

"It's too late. We have to keep going."

"No, Sophie, I don't want to!" the little girl shouted through her sobs.

Sophie turned to face Marie-Ève and suddenly slapped her. She grabbed her arm roughly. "Quit whining and follow me! We have to keep on!" Sophie hissed, pulling her along the path.

They continued another ten minutes or so before reaching a clearing where they caught sight of an old, dilapidated cabin; it looked like the area was a sugar bush.

"Come over here!" Sophie ordered.

Marie-Ève followed her. She was a pitiful sight. They walked by several rusty, old farm tools scattered randomly on the ground around the cabin. It was obvious that the place hadn't been used for several years. In the shed on one side of the cabin, logs seemed to have been thrown carelessly on the floor, amidst leaky pots. Sophie slowly pushed open the door of the cabin that winced and creaked ominously. Marie-Ève sidled up to Sophie.

"Have you been here before? In this place?"

Sophie didn't reply. A musty odour greeted them. The inside of the cabin had been vandalized several times; that was clear from the number of broken tiles and window panes. Only a long wooden table, the kind that used to be found in boarding school dining halls, was still standing on his own. Sophie went into the main room and came back with a lit candle stub. She led Marie-Ève towards a trap door that had been cut out of the floor.

"Now I'm going to show you where the ghosts come and kill baby kittens."

Marie-Ève was torn between the fear of having disobeyed her mother and the unhealthy curiosity to learn her friend's secret. Sophie leaned over, pulled on a metal ring, and tried to open the heavy trap door.

"Here – take the candle. You go first down the ladder."

Marie-Ève hesitated a moment, but could see that Sophie was using all her strength to hold the trap door open.

"Hurrrrry! I can't hold on much longer!"

Feeling helpless, Marie-Ève tentatively reached her foot down towards the first rung of the ladder. A few moments later, she had disappeared into the cellar. Sophie let go of the heavy door.

"Sophiiiiie!"

Sophie Ménard smiled widely, and wiped her dusty hands on her dirty dress, and turned towards Coconut.

"Here, kitty kitty kitty!"

*

It was only early in the evening, after endless discussions with the police chief, that Catherine and Barbara finally decided to continue searching on the other side of the pond.

"Come on, now. Marie-Ève would never have crossed the pond of her own accord!" Catherine kept repeating. "She knew it wasn't allowed!"

Dubuc shrugged his shoulders.

"We can't ignore the evidence. We've looked all over the campground and this side of the pond. Maybe your little girl couldn't resist the temptation to cross it. Especially when these flat rocks make the idea almost inviting. I suggest going over there."

One by one, they tiptoed over the rosary of rocks that took them to the other side of the pond. Five minutes later, Dubuc stopped and picked up three half-dead wildflowers and handed them over to Catherine. "It looks like the girls might have come through here."

Confident they were on the right track now, they pushed ahead more eagerly. They marched with determination into the fields, while the dusky sunlight lowered itself quickly into the far end of the lake. When they reached the edge of the forest, they stopped for a moment to take stock of the situation. Dubuc looked at his watch.

"It's already seven-thirty. It'll be dark soon. I say we should keep going for one more hour. After that, we'll have to call it quits. We can organize a search party first thing tomorrow morning if we have to."

Hearing these words, Catherine picked up her pace.

"No way. I'm not going home until I've found Marie-Ève!" she shouted.

The trio went into the forest and soon discovered the cabin in the sugar bush. Without saying a word, they were all thinking the same thing. They hoped the girls had found shelter there. About fifteen metres from the sugar bush, the police officer stopped again and crouched down. In the underbrush that rarely saw the sunlight, the dark, damp soil kept footprints as securely as a plaster mold. Dubuc took out his flashlight and shone it on the dull ground at their feet. Catherine and Barbara leaned over his shoulder.

"Look at this!" he exclaimed, pushing apart some vines. "There are two sets of footprints: little shoes and bigger running shoes. Marie-Ève and Sophie."

He stood up, motioned to them to stay back, and went

into the sugar shack. The cabin was dark and seemed to be deserted. As a precautionary measure, he pulled out his revolver and carefully walked towards the door. When he put his hand on the knob, he could feel a heavy lock pushing back in the half-light. The policeman stepped back from the door, made a tour of the building and set to work breaking a rickety window frame. To his great surprise, Catherine and Barbara had joined him.

"I just told you to . . . "

"Later," said Catherine in a determined tone.

She picked up a long branch lying on the ground and began hitting the window frame with a desperate energy. A moment later, they managed to hoist themselves into the cabin, one by one.

"What's that funny smell?" Barbara asked as soon as she was inside.

Chief Dubuc was walking around the main room, his nose sniffing the air.

"Burning wax. Someone was in here, and it wasn't very long ago."

Under Catherine and Barbara's astonished eyes, he crouched down on the dirty floor and ran his hand over the surface. He continued until he found what he was looking for.

"Come here," he told them.

"What in the world . . . ?" Catherine asked, her voice frantic now.

He stood up and opened his hand. In his palm were drops of dried wax. Red wax. He looked at the two women, pleased with his discovery. But to his dismay, Catherine grabbed hold of him and broke down into tears.

At times like this, Roméo Dubuc fell apart. He didn't know what to do. Overwhelmed with emotion himself, all he could do was to tap Catherine gently on the shoulder and mutter whatever stupid banalities he could think of to try to console her.

"You're right, we have to keep on," she said, as Barbara put a comforting arm around her shoulder. "Where did you find that red wax?"

"Right here, in front of the trap door," said Dubuc. "To tell you the truth, I was looking for it."

He leaned over again and tried to lift up the heavy trap door. This time, the strong odour of burning candles invaded the room. Just as he was about to go down the makeshift ladder, the policeman reached in his pocket for his flashlight, reassured by the touch of the cold metal revolver.

It was as if every step he took down the old ladder made the whole building crack. When his foot finally touched down on the ground, he pointed his flashlight straight out in front of him.

At first glance, the room vaguely reminded him of the basement of the old Protestant church where satanic rituals had been held. The policeman could recognize the little table, low and square, angled to the west, as well as the little copper vessels containing red wax, placed on each of the four corners of the table.

"Bingo!" he said to himself.

"Are you okay?" Catherine asked. She poked her head in the opening of the trap door.

Dubuc turned around, smiled at her and reached for his gun. But his gesture, which was meant to reassure her, didn't fool anyone. The cellar, built right on the soil, measured about three metres by four. All of the policeman's attention suddenly focused on a large, round burlap sack on the ground at the back of the room. He walked towards it, his mind suddenly invaded by doubt.

"Can we come down too?" Catherine asked.

"No!" he answered, brusquely, as he continued towards the canvas bag.

Dubuc noticed his shirt was soaked, stained with the sweat that also covered his face. But he realized it was his own fear that was making him perspire. He stood still for a moment, looking down at the dark heap at his feet, unable to move an inch or to touch it.

Then, drawing on the last of his energy, he lifted up the sack from the ground, undid the string knotted around its opening and dumped out its contents.

Black robes.

He breathed a sigh of relief, then turned towards the trap door.

"False alarm, Ladies. Everything is fine. I'm coming back up."

At the very instant he lifted his foot to first rung on the ladder, he caught sight of a small pool of blood behind it. His nerves tightened and he aimed his flashlight towards it.

*

When Roméo Dubuc finally emerged from the cellar, his face livid, he carried in his arms the dead body of Coconut, horribly mutilated and drained of blood. At this horrific sight, Catherine buried her face in her hands and Barbara began to scream hysterically. Even though he normally couldn't find his tongue on this sort of occasion, he knew exactly what to say.

"Let's get out of here. There's nothing more to be done in this place," he said, pulling the two women close to him.

Chapter 12

When he left the sugar bush, Chief Dubuc left Catherine and Barbara alone for a moment and, to satisfy his conscience, he cast the beam of his flashlight around the building one last time. What he discovered gave him a new burst of energy.

"Come here! Quick!"

He crouched down and showed them what he had found.

"Footprints. The same ones we saw a minute ago, when we got here, but going in the opposite direction."

"Marie-Ève was alive when she left here! Thank goodness!" exclaimed Catherine, clasping her hands together.

"Let's hope so. But look down here. Next to the girls' footprints, there's another set that are going in the same direction."

He pointed his flashlight close to the ground. "An adult's footprints."

Catherine made a superhuman effort to gather her thoughts and retain her presence of mind. She didn't want her emotions to cloud her judgment. "So you think an adult met the girls here? Maybe a hunter, or a farmer."

"Or someone who was waiting for them," said Dubuc, solemnly. "Look. The footsteps start at the other side of the sugar bush."

He suddenly realized that they were in almost complete darkness.

"As soon as we get back, I'm going to supply the Sûreté with their description so that the cops can keep an eye on the spot on Route 124 where there's a bit of a clearing in the woods. But we'll have to wait until tomorrow morning to get on with our search."

They went back the way they had come in and soon reached the campground. Usually hidden under the awning of the tent, a shadowy figure stood about fifteen metres away from them. Dubuc was the first to notice it. He moved towards it, keeping some distance between himself and two women, circled the tent under the cover of the trees and arrived behind the stranger. He was now only two metres away from the shadow. But just when he was about to pull out his gun, the smell of cheap cologne wafted up to his nostrils. He put his .38 back in its holster and laid his hand on Jerry Ménard's shoulder.

Jerry turned around with a strident scream that nailed Catherine and Barbara to the ground.

"Mercy, you gave me a scare! Your deputy called me to tell me that Sophie had disappeared!"

"Yes, that's true. Your daughter and Marie-Ève have been missing since this afternoon," the police officer stated calmly. "We have a bit of an idea about where they've been, but we'll have to organize a search party tomorrow morning."

Catherine approached him and said, "We have to keep our hopes up. We've found some footprints."

But she didn't finish her sentence, because, without warning, Roméo Dubuc's enormous left foot plunked itself down on hers.

The policeman put a fatherly arm around Ménard's shoulders and took him aside. "Trust us, Jerry, we'll do everything in our power and more to find the little girls. If Sophie comes back in the meantime, give us a call, all right? Promise?"

"Promise!" Ménard declared, tracing the sign of the cross on his chest. "The little devil. I've been turning Chesterville upside down for the past three hours, trying to find her."

As Ménard was leaving, Dubuc caught up to him. "By the way, what size shoe do you wear, Jerry?"

"Who, me?" He thought about it for a second. "8½. What for?"

"Just wondering."

When the police officer came back to where she was standing, Catherine was biting her lip. "I guess I made a boo-boo."

"Almost, but never mind. Jerry seemed pretty sincere, but there's nothing that says he couldn't have planned the 'disappearance' of his own little girl as a red herring to distract the police. He's quite capable of that sort of thing, that beast. At any rate, the footprints we saw next to the girls seem pretty close to Jerry's size. I'll take a cast of the prints tomorrow morning."

But at this point Catherine was only listening with one ear. Dubuc could tell the events of the day had exhausted her.

"Come on, pack up your things, Ladies, and say goodbye to camping," he told them. "What with Marie-Ève and Sophie missing, it wouldn't be safe to leave you alone here. You can spend the night with Solange, my wife's sister, and get some rest. We'll start our search again tomorrow morning, first thing. Six o'clock."

⋆

Roméo Dubuc was driving home when a warm and sleepy feeling came over him, and he was afraid he might lose control of his car. He slammed on the brake: Toto Grimaldi! He had forgotten all about him! With a squeal of the tires, he made a U-turn, turned on the siren and put the accelerator to the floor as he headed for the cemetery. Toto, in spite of himself, had been a witness to the satanic ceremony. His testimony was likely to be a precious help to their investigation.

He got to the cemetery about ten minutes later and checked his watch: ten-forty p.m. The street was dark and deserted. He had no trouble finding the modest home of the Grimaldis, which wasn't kept up very well. Lucien's patrol car was parked out in front. Dubuc felt relieved. His deputy had obviously decided to keep an eye on everything. He went up to the house and knocked at the door. No answer. Odd, he thought. He stepped back and glanced up at the second floor. A lamp was on, dimly lighting up one of the bedrooms that looked out on the street. He knocked again. This time, he caught a glimpse of a shadow which furtively pulled back the drapes and opened the door. It was Lucette Grimaldi. A cigarette hanging out her mouth, dressed in a mauve satin nightgown that couldn't hide her sagging chest, Toto's wife spoke as though she were chewing on her words. The fact that her husband had been isolated since the previous night seemed to have pushed her over the edge of her nerves.

"Roméo! It's about time! It's unliveable. Unbearable. Toto's gone and holed himself up in his room with the coffee machine. Don't want to talk to no one but you. Hurry up! Get up there and talk to him, would you?"

"Have you talked to him tonight?" asked Dubuc, going up the stairs to the second floor.

"Him? No way! He don't want to have anything to do with me. I just took some sandwiches up there, for supper. It's like talking to a wall!"

"You have to understand, Lucette. Since last night, your husband has been in real danger. Of course that's hard on his nerves."

"Yeah, that's just what Lucien was saying. Seems Toto recognized the voices he heard in the graveyard."

"Did he mention any names?" asked Dubuc, his interest piqued.

"Nope. He said he'd only talk to you. Don't trust another soul. Not even his wife!"

She returned to the kitchen, muttering a litany of insults as she went.

Dubuc went upstairs into the bedroom where the cemetery caretaker had barricaded himself.

"Toto, it's me, Roméo Dubuc. You can open up now."

No answer.

"Open the door, Toto!"

Lucette was at the bottom of the staircase.

"Maybe he's finally gone to sleep," she suggested, leaning her elbow up against the bannister.

The smell of burnt coffee that filled the upper floor raised the police officer's suspicions. He stiffened and braced himself, and then plunged his shoulder into the door, which gave way easily under the heavy thud.

Toto Grimaldi had collapsed on the carpet, his face haggard and his head resting on the edge of the bed. The police chief hurried to his side. The man was breathing with great difficulty and his vital signs were weak. The rug around him was stained with vomit. He had obviously tried to grab hold of the sheets to lift himself up, but hadn't been able to manage. For the police officer, the yellowed complexion, chilly skin and absence of motion left no doubt about the method used to silence Toto Grimaldi.

"Call an ambulance, Lucette! Right away! Tell them to get ready to pump his stomach!"

When the ambulance had left, Dubuc proceeded to inspect the property. Despite his efforts, he couldn't find any evidence in the room. But he was convinced that the satanic cult had tried to poison Toto. Lucette stood in the doorway, her eyes wide with fright.

"Do you think he's going to make it, Roméo? Do you think so?"

"You'll have to pray for him, my poor Lucette. And wait to find out how badly the poison has damaged his internal organs. Your husband is lucky to be alive. I've also asked them to put a guard on duty at his hospital room, as a precaution."

He picked up a ham sandwich with the tips of his fingers. "Believe me, there's enough arsenic in this to put the whole twenty-second regiment to sleep! The guys who planned this little episode definitely wanted to shut his trap for the rest of eternity."

He suddenly turned to Lucette. "Do you have any idea where the poison could have come from?"

She shrugged her shoulders, avoiding his glance.

"Come on, try to think. This is important."

"We haven't been out all day."

"Have you had any company? I don't know, maybe a delivery man, a neighbour, the tax man, anyone? That poison didn't land in your sandwiches by itself. Think, Lucette. It must have got here somehow."

Dubuc led her by the hand down the stairs and over towards the refrigerator. Realizing that he was about to empty out its contents, Lucette Grimaldi seemed to suddenly remember something. "I didn't feel like cooking tonight," she finally admitted. "Especially since I'd been given these sandwiches."

"My, my! And who would have given them to you?"

"It was Lorraine Talbot. She brought them over here around five o'clock. She knew how bad my nerves were. I didn't want anything to eat, but I took the plate up to Toto."

Dubuc tried to reach Lucien by radio to tell him what was going on, but there was no answer. He rushed outside. The patrol car was still parked in front of the Grimaldis' house. No one could be seen inside. The policeman reached for his gun and moved, carefully and quietly, towards the car. He discovered Lucien spread out on the front seat, wrapped in a strong odour of chloroform.

The policeman shook his deputy until he came back to his senses.

"You've been gassed, Lucien. What happened?"

"A woman . . . a redhead with sunglasses . . . she leaned into the window to talk to me. I guess her accomplice took me from behind."

Dubuc briefed him quickly on the recent developments. "It's pretty obvious they chloroformed you to clear the way tonight. And I'd swear that the visitor with the red wig was Lorraine Talbot, and that Jules got you from behind. The Talbots are in the cult right up to their necks, Old Boy. To get rid of the witness who was getting in their way, they brought sandwiches laced with arsenic to Toto and chloroform to put you to sleep. Nice of them, eh?"

"Maybe the Talbots missed out on Toto, but they seem to have been successful with J.A. and Conrad," replied Lucien, back to his own self.

"If you're right, it's the proof that any means justify the ends of the cult. A stabbing, a faked suicide, kidnapping two little girls, poison. These people will stop at nothing!"

"How's he doing?" asked Lucien.

"Toto? More dead than alive right now. The poison has already started working unfortunately. I didn't say so to Lucette, but the prognosis doesn't look too good."

The police officer checked his watch.

"Well, anyway. Go home and rest a while. We have to start up the search for Marie-Ève and Sophie again, first thing tomorrow morning. And I need you at the office. Meanwhile, I'm going off to pay the Talbots a little visit."

★

His inspection of the area around the grocery store confirmed the policeman's suspicions that he was wasting his time. The van wasn't in the garage, the place was dark, and all the doors were locked. There was no sign of Pauline or her brothers. The nest was empty.

Roméo Dubuc put out a search bulletin to the regional office of the Sûreté, supplying the police with a detailed description of Jules and Lorraine Talbot. He made sure that a watch was put on their house, in case the suspects came back during the night. Then he went home to try to catch a few hourse of sleep. It was past two o'clock in the morning.

As he walked by his son's bedroom, his attention was drawn to a little white candle burning on André's dresser and casting a shimmering shadow on the walls. It was Gilberte's vigil, her way of keeping alive the memory of their adoptive son who had died two years before. The police officer came in for a few minutes to gather his spirits. The room had been left untouched. Nothing had changed since André's death. His brass bed was still placed in the back of the room, near the window, and his pine desk was still covered with papers. On the shelf above it, several athletic medals and trophies stood in a row. But, closer to the door, there was evidence of André's more recent interests: terrifying posters of heavy metal groups, their members draped in black leather and chains, brandishing devilish makeup and posed obscenely. Dubuc had tried hard to overcome his disgust for this period of his son's life, the months leading up to his tragic death. A little black and white photo was discretely stuck underneath one of the posters. It showed

André with Liette Bardois, the girl he was with on the night of his death. A strange young woman, the policeman said to himself. She had been questioned briefly during the investigation into André's death, and then she had disappeared from the area. Dubuc had no idea what had become of her since then.

On the dresser, the flame of the little candle had started to flicker. Dubuc went and blew it out, then left the room.

*

The police officer got to the Green Valley Campground at five-thirty in the morning. The darkness seemed to want to persist, but a glimpse of daylight was making a valiant effort to rise above the horizon. Three officers from the Sûreté, accompanied by a tracking dog, had already arrived, and so had Catherine, Barbara and Marguerita Bussières. Catherine had obviously not been able to shut her eyes all night. She had spent the evening recruiting a dozen campers for the search party.

Dubuc walked over to his colleagues and spread out a detailed map of the surroundings for them to see.

"I'm almost sure the girls left the cabin in the sugar bush in the company of an adult," he told them. "At least, that's what the footprints seem to suggest. You didn't catch any of the suspects last night?"

One of the officers assured him that no adult accompanied by two girls had passed the police barricade the previous night.

"That leaves us with two possibilities," Dubuc declared, "One, they're still in the area; or two, they've had lots of time to get out of here."

They agreed to split up. The policeman and the dog

would go over the western section of the site and the others would spread out in little teams of three or four over the rest of the area, enabling the search party to coordinate their efforts effectively. Dubuc repeated the instructions to each person, one after the other, before he joined the women.

"Meet back here at noon!" he shouted out to the group.

The teams hiked over to the other bank of the river, across from the campground. The police chief's group hadn't advanced more than three hundred steps before they heard shouts behind them. It was Jerry Ménard. He was running towards them, breathless and soaking in sweat.

"You want to come with us?" asked Dubuc. "You look more like you're off to a wedding."

The sector Dubuc had chosen was a rather sloping and rocky spot, and Marguerita Bussières was not amused.

"I don't want to complain," she repeated many times to the others, "but this is a bit much. If I knew we were going mountain climbing I would have dressed for the occasion!"

Dubuc couldn't help but smile at the woman's coquettish manner. Jerry Ménard, for his part, didn't fare much better. He was wearing expensive Italian leather loafers, and was making his way on tiptoe, as though walking on eggs.

"Stop acting like a fruitcake, Jerry. We don't have all day, you know!" Dubuc shouted at him, impatient.

"All right already!" Jerry retorted, picking up his pace.

Ménard hadn't noticed how swampy the ground was. He suddenly realized that he had plunged his foot several centimetres down into the muck, and that water was filling up his fine leather shoes. Worse, he then fell face-first onto the wet grass.

The others hadn't missed a thing. The group broke out into hilarious laughter, and couldn't make a move to help him.

"Come on, Guys, give me a hand! You useless twits!" Jerry moaned, floundering like a hooked fish.

Dubuc was the first person to reach out to him. He stood Jerry back up on his feet and started to look for his shoes that had sunk deeply into the swamp water. After a few minutes of looking, he announced:

"Here they are." He held them up, proudly exhibiting his treasure to their owners.

Ménard grumbled as he lagged behind for a few moments, but soon caught up to the group.

At around ten o'clock, they had only covered three kilometres. The police chief couldn't help but notice that Catherine was growing more worried by the minute. He couldn't blame her. The latest information from the other groups, relayed by radio, weren't any more encouraging. No sign of Marie-Ève and Sophie anywhere on the site.

Dubuc refused to admit it, to himself or anyone else, but he knew all too well that in these kinds of searches the first twenty-four hours after the disappearance were crucial. That was the time the trail was still fresh and the clues were still visible.

The police officer continued to trudge ahead, eyeing Marguerita every once in a while. J.A.'s widow clearly viewed the search party as an occasion to show off her new suit. She walked slowly and painfully, one hand on her straw hat and the other arm swinging like a pendulum. What role had this woman played in her husband's death? Dubuc wondered again. His first instinct had been to suspect her. A normal reaction.

After all, Marguerita had won on several accounts. She'd got a hefty inheritance, vengeance and freedom to start her life all over again. And her alibi was about as fragile as a porcelain tea cup. Dubuc didn't believe the story about her affair with the chauffeur, Roland Fafard. On the other hand, he could hardly imagine Marguerita stabbing her husband or strangling Conrad. The woman may have had a strong character, but all the same . . .

As they walked back to their starting point, around noon, the silence was heavy. As far as they could see, the other teams hadn't come across any clues either. Not even the police dog had been able to sniff out anything; his efforts had been hampered by a strong wind blowing in the wrong direction. They didn't have anything new to go on.

"We'll get a helicopter up in a couple of hours!" announced the police sergeant from the Sûreté, when he got off the phone.

Dubuc turned towards Catherine and crossed his fingers, wishing them luck. But she was too spent to even react.

*

"I guess the emotional stuff doesn't take away your appetite!" exclaimed Lucien, seeing the police chief sprinkle grated cheese all over a huge plate of spaghetti.

"If I was bothered by emotion, I would've starved to death a long time ago!"

"Do you think the helicopter will manage to find something everyone else missed this morning?"

"Who knows? The adult that was with Marie-Ève and Sophie had lots of time to get out of sight last night. Don't forget that more than two hours went by between the time we found the footprints and the time the police set up their checkpoint at the edge of the woods, there, on the highway."

The policeman abruptly pushed his plate aside.

"You know as well as I do that there haven't ever been kidnappings around here before. But yesterday, bang! Two at the same time."

"Do you think the kidnapper might ask for a ransom?"

"I don't want to disappoint you, but I doubt it. A kidnapper who's after a ransom makes sure he snatches children with parents who can afford to pay it. And, you know, Jerry isn't made of money, and Catherine Gagnon doesn't seem to be particularly rich either. If you ask me, Lucien, this kidnapping has nothing to do with money."

Lucien Langlois knew his boss well enough that he had already thought all this through. Dubuc got up, shuffled things around in the cupboard and came back with an old book. When he blew on the cover, a cloud of dust filled the room.

"Yesterday, I paid a little visit to our parish priest, Louis Patenaude. That poor man, saint that he is, has already had his wine cellar pillaged twice and he finally decided to ask for some security. While I was having a cup of coffee, I glanced at his bookcase. Mighty impressive! A very learned man, our priest is. And a collector of rare books: old editions of Baudelaire, Hugo, Flaubert and the whole gang. But this too."

The chief placed the antique book between the hands of his deputy, who read the title: *Calendar of Christian and Pagan Rituals of the Modern Era.*

Dubuc continued.

"According to Father Louis, the book was written in 1928 by a Jesuit from France. What really caught my attention was a little chapter on 'Satanic Festivals and Rituals.' It talks about satanic cults in the United States, how they get together every summer, in July, for the full moon, to honour Satan. It's sort of like their own New Year's Eve, a big tradition. But it's also called the 'Fire Rite to the Lord of the Underworld.' A barbaric and primitive ceremony, inspired by the ritual practices of the ancient Incas, with human sacrifice and the whole bit."

Lucien tried to force himself to take a breath, but couldn't.

"Did you really say *human* sacrifices?"

"Oh, yeah, that's what I said."

Lucien gulped his saliva again.

"You must be kidding."

"Not one bit. If what this book says is true, I'd guess Marie-Ève and Sophie have front-row tickets in the balcony, if you know what I mean."

Chapter 13

Early in the afternoon, the following day, the Sûreté contacted Roméo Dubuc, but the news wasn't what he had hoped for.

"Still nothing," he whispered to Catherine, still holding the receiver. "What? Yes, that's right, the name is Liette Bardois. I've got it. Thanks, Boys."

"Something new?"

"No, but the Sûreté has traced the steps of that girl who was with André the night of his death," Dubuc said, excitedly. "I've been trying to track her down for two years. She lives three-quarters of an hour away from here."

He headed straight for the next village, St. Jérémie. His informer had told him that Liette Bardois, who also went by the name Liette Grondin, had a baby and lived on social assistance in a rooming house in the village. But there was something that interested Dubuc even more. Apparently this girl had been J.A. Bussières's mistress for a while, shortly after André's death.

The dilapidated house was located in the old part of St. Jérémie, near the CN yards. Dubuc checked the address again and went up to the door of Room number 7 on the ground floor. A child's crying filtered out from under the door. He knocked again, several tries. The girl who came to open the door carried her miserable circumstances like dirt on her face. Her green eyes were dull, and she looked as if her youth had prematurely left her. Her blond hair was filthy and fell into her face in messy tendrils. Still, there was no mistaking that she was the same girl as in the photo on André's desk. Liette Bardois jumped when she saw the policeman at the door.

"How did you find me?" she asked nervously.

"Oh, I'm a stubborn old mule! You're calling yourself Liette Grondin now, to cover your tracks?"

"Why would I do that? I've got nothing to hide."

Roméo Dubuc brandished the black cat fetish under her nose.

"And I suppose this is a St. Joseph's medal, mmm? We found it in André's pocket the night he died."

Liette Bardois lowered her eyes and let him into the room.

"André was the nicest fellow in the world. He was wasting his time with me. But he loved me, you know."

"Were you in that organization? The satanic cult?"

"No. His death was just a stupid accident. The other kids we hung out with, they were just like us. On welfare or pogey. André got pissed out of his skull at a party. When three guys came in at about eleven with pills, they made an idiotic bet."

"What kind of a bet?"

"Whoever could swallow the most pills without getting sick."

"Come on, Liette. You're pulling my leg."

"No, I swear. It's true. Then André fell into a coma. You know the rest of the story."

The police chief pushed his head back and leaned up against the wall, struggling with the emotions and memories that had haunted him since the death of his son. Liette watched him, never flinching, hugging her child closer to her.

"You were J.A. Bussières's mistress. Did you know he was the leader of the cult too?" asked Dubuc.

"I found that out not long after I left him. I was with him for a year. It was after André's death and I was sick of life. To the point I was thinking of killing myself. J.A.

bought me pretty clothes, jewellery. He gave me back my will to live. But he never talked to me about that organization. He always said that the walls had ears."

"The cult has kidnapped two little girls and I've got to find them. Every minute counts. Their lives are probably in danger. I found out that a barbaric ritual is supposed to take place on the full moon in July, which means tomorrow night, Friday."

"You mean the 'Fire Rite to the Lord of the Underworld?'" asked Liette. "J.A. mentioned that."

"You talked about it?" exclaimed the policeman, astonished.

"Not exactly, but J.A. talked in his sleep. When I'd ask him the next morning, he was always embarrassed to talk about it. He said I'd never be able to understand anyway."

"Can you tell me anything else about it?" Dubuc's eagerness was visible.

She shook her shoulders, and her fatigue showed. "J.A. said it was a purification ceremony, a ritual of cleansing by fire. In honour of Satan. That kind of thing. Poor guy, when he dreamed of that cult, he always woke up soaking wet, he sweated so hard."

"I need to know where the ceremony takes place, Liette. We don't have much time left."

"J.A. did mention once that the 'Fire Rite' was always held in 'the place where the full moon penetrates granite.' That's what he said."

"What's this gibberish?" asked Dubuc, incredulous.

"That's all I can tell you."

Dubuc left Liette Bardois, feeling more puzzled than ever. The words of his son's former girlfriend played over and over again in his mind: "The place where the full moon penetrates granite.'

He had no idea where that place could be. On the other

hand, he knew all too well that the moon would be full the following night.

*

Coming back from the Police Station, Dubuc found himself nose-to-nose with Jeannot Lejeune. The chief glared in Lucien's direction, but his deputy just shrugged.

"To what do I owe the honour of your visit?" asked the chief with false courtesy. Lejeune was used to it.

Lejeune's mottled purplish complexion and his raging eyes didn't fool anybody. His pit-bull temperament went right for the jugular, as usual. "I need some advice, Chief," he said. "How do you spell 'incompetent'? It's for my next article on the local police investigation."

For Dubuc, that was the drop that made the bucket overflow. He grabbed Lejeune firmly by his jacket, lifted him up off the ground like a matchstick and planted his shoulders up against the wall.

"Okay, wise Guy. I've been putting up with your moron face way too long. I think it's time I have some fun with you."

He waved his fist under the reporter's nose. Lejeune realized too late that he had crossed the line. Lucien came between them just in time. The two opponents stayed there, face to face, ashamed and remorseful about their ridiculous behaviour. It was Dubuc who suggested they call off the argument. "Look, Jeannot. Time is running out. For once, you could be of use to us. I've got an idea. We absolutely have to trap the cult and I need the *Clarion* to help. I've found out that there's going to be a big satanic ceremony tomorrow night. Friday. Your weekend edition should be out just in time in the morning. With your help, we can save two little girls from a very probable death. Can I count on you?"

Lejeune didn't move. His square jaw jutted out; he was measuring the consequences of his decision.

"The *Clarion* is nobody's slave, and certainly not yours! But if the two girls are in trouble, well, sure, we'll do whatever you want."

They shook hands for the first time in years, and Dubuc took him into his office. They only got out late in the afternoon.

★

The special edition of the *Clarion Express* was circulated to all the households in Chesterville at eight o'clock the next morning. Dubuc was already in his office at six, and two hours later was fuming with impatience. Lucien brought him a copy of the newspaper as soon as it arrived. The article that interested him was on the front page, under a photo of the two missing girls, and the headline was in large bold red type. It read:

Disappearance of Two Young Girls:
The Police are Hot on the Trail

Jeannot Lejeune – New development in the case of the disappearance of the two girls, Marie-Ève Gagnon and Sophie Ménard, who were reported missing after not returning home last Tuesday night in Chesterville. At the time this issue went to press, the *Clarion Express* had just learned that it would appear to be a kidnapping case involving the acts of a satanic cult based in the U.S.A., apparently active in the area around Chesterville. M.-È. Gagnon, six years old, and S. Ménard, ten years old, appear to have gone missing near an abandoned cabin in the sugar bush, on the bank of the river across from Green Valley Campground. According to local police, every indication is that the members of the local cult will perform their annual satanic rituals which are said to be of a barbaric nature. The police fears for the lives of these two girls and asks the community to keep a close eye out. Police will patrol possible cult gathering places, such as the cemetery and the abandoned Protestant church. Last Wednesday, a thorough search by police and volunteers, as well as a police dog and a helicopter from the Sûreté du Québec, failed to turn up any evidence. The police are still hopeful they will find the two little girls alive.

"Perfect!" exclaimed Dubuc, folding the paper up on his desk. "Lejeune did what he needed to do. With an article like that, we know that the cult will stay a long way away from the cemetery and the old Protestant church. Let's see what happens next."

What happened next was a door slamming, five minutes later. Catherine Gagnon bounded into the office, beyond herself, waving the newspaper under their nose.

"With an article like this, you can be sure the cult will move on or cancel its plans, and we'll never see Marie-Ève again! Good work! Really, I can't believe I trusted you to find the girls, Dubuc. You aren't worth any more than any other stupid country cop!"

She threw down the newspaper and looked down at the policeman with such disgust that he was afraid she might spit in his face. She turned on her heels and was about to leave the way she came in when he intercepted her.

"Just a moment, Catherine. Sit down, would you? I'll explain everything."

She was startled to see him in control of the situation, and of himself.

"I hesitated to tell you about it before, and that's my own fault. But all the clues point to the same thing. We had to take a big risk tonight and that's what I did. Don't wait for anyone to ask for a ransom, Catherine, it won't happen. Anyway, if that's what it was about, the kidnapper would have already got in touch with you. The girls have been missing for two and a half days. That's too long for it to be about money. We have to look the situation in the eye. It's obvious this thing's been carefully planned: no clues, no trail except for the footprints near the cabin in the sugar bush and the ones going into the woods."

"How do you explain it then?" Catherine said, impatiently. "The girls can't have turned into fawns!"

"I can understand your frustration, believe me. The Sûreté can't explain it either. Personally, I'm convinced the kidnapping was successful because the local population is in on it."

"What in the world do you mean?"

"Let's say the cult has its roots in Chesterville. It probably does. In that case, it's a lot easier for them to cover their tracks. People know each other, they're used to living together and working together, to keeping an eye on the neighbourhood, to hiding the clues, to getting the kids out of the area, all those things that they do after their satanic ceremonies anyway."

His logic impressed Catherine. "You're a quick study, I'd say. A few days ago you didn't know anything about the satanic movement."

In other circumstances, the compliment would have made him puff out his chest in pride, but today the police officer had no impulse to enjoy the moment.

"And I have to tell you something, Catherine. It's very likely that Sophie Ménard is directly involved in the kidnapping of your daughter."

She was obviously startled.

"That's the conclusion I'd draw at the moment," he continued. "The inspectors from the Sûreté have gone over the footprints on the other side of the river with a fine-toothed comb. Marie-Ève seems to have stalled for a bit, as though she was getting ready to turn around. But Sophie didn't hesitate for one second. Her tracks lead directly to the cabin in the sugar bush."

"Are you trying to suggest that Sophie may have deliberately led my daughter to the cult?"

Roméo Dubuc was too uneasy to answer her.

*

At around three o'clock in the afternoon, the police station was invaded with a dozen plainclothes police officers from the Sûreté du Québec, St. Jérémie detachment. Lucien served coffee while the chief invited them into his office. He had used every power of persuasion he could summon to convince the administration of the Sûreté that the fate of the two little girls was linked to the satanic ceremony planned for that evening.

Dubuc went up to the large-scale military map of the Chesterville area and pointed at it with his finger.

"If the *Clarion* article has the results I predict it will, the members of the cult will avoid the cemetery and the old Protestant church like the plague."

"Do you want us to send some people to both places anyway?" one officer asked.

"Just one of the men as a precaution," replied Dubuc.

"What is going to stop them from cancelling the ceremony completely, because of the newspaper article?" another one asked.

Dubuc held up the old book with its yellowed, dusty cover. "Tradition, that's what. This book I got from the parish priest says that members of this satanic cult have kept up this custom for centuries. That's what makes me believe they'll perform their ritual somewhere tonight. They have to. But where?"

One of the police officers, who was a full head taller than the others, went up to the police chief.

"Roméo, we don't know anything about the cult you're talking about or the way it works. You claim that it's directly involved with the two murders and a near-fatal poisoning attempt, but you were forced to release your only suspect in this case. I would really like to believe you, but the evidence isn't very strong."

"No, I couldn't hold Jules Talbot," Dubuc was forced to admit. "There wasn't sufficient proof. Even if we found his prints all over the weapon used for the crime. The problem is that there were other prints impossible to identify. This said, we have learned since then that Jules is part of the cult. He and his wife tried to poison Toto Grimaldi, the caretaker of the cemetery, and only last Tuesday night, they chloroformed my deputy, Lucien. Then they vanished. They haven't been seen since."

He threw his hands up in the air, as if he was trying to coax them along.

"I know what you're thinking, Boys. You're thinking: careful, Roméo! No apparent motive, no proof, no witness! But that's the whole problem with a satanic cult! Their motives and their methods are completely different from those of other criminals, so the usual kind of police investigation doesn't turn anything up. I'll admit it: we're dealing with a bunch of people who aren't afraid of anything. It's a well-oiled machine, their organization, and the members of the cult are used to working together and covering each other's backsides. We don't have much of an idea of their practices. That gives them a huge head start on us. On the other hand, I'm still convinced that J.A. Bussières's killer and his son Conrad's killer are the same person. Two much evidence leads to the same guy. Our only chance to get rid of them for good is to dismantle the cult, by capturing them in the act. Tonight!"

"Where do you want me to post my men?" asked the sergeant who was a head taller than the others.

"I'd love to know for sure," retorted Dubuc. "All we know is that the ceremony is supposed to be performed 'in the place where the full moon penetrates granite.'"

The phrase drew a hearty round of laughter from the officers. Dubuc ignored them, and continued, "If we rely on this information, then we head to the two places there's granite. One's in the cemetery and one's in the old Protestant church. Those are the two places where the people who belong to the cult know they're going to be watched. So tonight they'll have to find another spot."

"Where do we post the other officers?" repeated the sergeant.

"The only logical place is the granite quarry near St. Jérémie, which is about a half-hour from Chesterville," said Dubuc.

"Logical but unlikely," interrupted Lucien. "Think about it for a second. The members of the cult won't feel much like leaving Chesterville when they know we're on their heels."

"Can you think of another place in Chesterville?"

Lucien shook his head. The sergeant from the Sûreté was getting more and more impatient.

"Roméo, we have six men at your service here. Do you want me to send them home?"

"No way!" retorted Dubuc. "No way. Tell them to patrol the area around the granite quarry after ten o'clock tonight. If they follow their traditions, the members of the cult should gather at the full moon at midnight. As planned, we'll be in contact by radio with your men at the cemetery and at the old church, and they'll come and give us a hand if we need them."

Dubuc sat down again, exhausted. His gaze was drawn to the amulet placed on his desk. He lowered his eyes.

Chapter 14

Dubuc's daydreams were interrupted by Lucien. "I want to join the cemetery team."

"You're supposed to be going to the granite quarry."

"I know, but I have a feeling they won't go there. Or to the cemetery or the old church either."

"You think the cult is going to cancel their ceremony, just to be on the safe side?"

"No, the tradition is too important. I'm convinced they'll perform their ritual tonight in Chesterville, but somewhere else. So just to make sure my conscience is clear, I'd rather hang around."

He went out.

Dubuc sat there for a while in his chair, his arms folded across his chest and his feet on his desk. For a brief moment, Conrad Bussières crossed his mind and he bound to his feet, tapping his forehead: "Of course! Why didn't I think of that before?"

He rushed out of the office and grabbed his deputy by the coat sleeve.

"Lucien, tonight you're going with me!"

"Where?"

"You'll know in due time. Right now, I'm going to go see Trépanier."

"He went out to supper with his men."

Dubuc caught up to him fifteen minutes later. Keeping his cards close to his chest, he asked the two policemen from the Sûreté to join them that night in Chesterville. The others would be posted elsewhere, as planned.

"I hope you know what you're doing," Sergeant Trépanier tossed out at him, as though he didn't really believe he did. "This isn't the time for playing hide and seek. If this ceremony is going to take place at the granite quarry, I'll need my men. I'll give you one officer. No more."

"That's better than nothing," said Dubuc, deciding not to argue. "Besides, who knows? It might be worth our while."

*

Dubuc, Lucien and Alain Rousseau, the officer assigned to them by the Sûreté, were the last ones to leave the police station that evening. Each of the four teams had decided to contact Trépanier's team, posted at the quarry, every half hour until midnight.

Lucien was surprised to see his boss drive directly to the psychiatric hospital.

"I'll explain later," he said.

He drove into the parking lot of the institution and parked the car discreetly. The three police officers headed for the fire escape, where there were stairs from each floor of the hospital leading outside. Dubuc went up first. They climbed up to the fourth floor before letting themselves into the hospital. They found themselves in a small, dimly-lit room with tables and chairs piled up along the walls.

"Do you think anyone saw us?" asked Lucien.

"I doubt it," replied Alain Rousseau. "It's as dark as the devil in here."

Dubuc couldn't keep from laughing. He pointed his index finger towards the full moon outside the window. "Speak of the devil . . . "

His watch stood at exactly ten-thirty p.m. He contacted the other team, as planned.

"Another hour and a half to wait," said the police chief.

"If there's anything to wait for," Lucien said, a little petulantly.

"Follow me."

Dubuc pulled the door part-way open. The hospital corridor was dark and deserted. They hugged the wall like shadows, holding their breath every time they heard a noise. As they walked by the large window in the games room, they sank to the floor and crawled to the end of the hallway. The unexpected arrival of an orderly sent them scurrying like rabbits. They opened the first door they found.

Lucien sneezed. "Shoot! It's a storage room for cleaning products. We've gotta get out of here, quick!"

They slid along the walls again, until Dubuc motioned to them to open the second door on their right. Now they were in a freshly-painted and empty wing of the hospital. Dubuc pushed the door open. It was the chapel. They went inside. The only light from the room seemed to come from the flickering flames on the Chinese lanterns hanging to their right, yet Lucien noticed that there was natural light inside the chapel. He raised his head. Through a small œil-de-bœuf window cut out of a superb granite wall at the back of the chapel, the glow of the full moon generously illuminated the room.

He turned back to look at the police chief, who was jubilant.

"'In the place where the full moon penetrates granite.'"

"How did you figure it out?"

"I came in here with Conrad, after he was admitted to the hospital. I just remembered that this afternoon."

Alain Rousseau reminded them about something more urgent. "It's nearly eleven-thirty p.m. I'm going to call the others and let them know where we are. Then we'll have to return to our posts as soon as we can. If this ceremony is really going to take place, it's going to happen soon." The three police officers cased the room quickly.

Except for the door they had come through, the only exit was behind the altar, on a little podium, and went into the vestry. Dubuc stationed himself close by. He was separated from the others by about fifteen rows of pews. Lucien and Alain Rousseau were hidden behind the double doors at the entrance, ready to jump into action at the signal.

At the very back of the chapel, a large clock slowly counted out the minutes and seconds. Dubuc raised his head. Ten minutes before midnight.

He was hunched over, behind the confessional booth. He took out his revolver and nervously checked that it was loaded.

There was utter silence. Only the monotone drone of the fan above their heads could be heard. Lucien was the first to react. The police chief noticed that he was making large gestures and looking at his watch. It was past midnight. Lucien crouched down and crawled past the pews to Dubuc.

"Do you hear that noise?" asked the deputy.

The chief cocked his ear. "It sounds like someone praying."

The sound became louder and louder, like a crowd in the distance approaching, and now filled the entire chapel. Alain Rousseau came over to them. Dubuc saw that he was sweating and could barely speak.

"Guys, do you hear that?"

Lucien stood up, his senses alerted and his body erect. He moved away from the others and slowly made his way through the chapel. Suddenly, he returned towards the two others and pointed at the floor. "They're right *underneath* us!"

Dubuc motioned to them to leave the chapel without making any noise. The three of them went into the vestry.

"We don't have a floor plan of the building. If we separate, we might get lost," said Lucien. "This hospital is a real maze of corridors."

"We'll have to make it up as we go along," replied Dubuc. "Follow me."

They left the vestry and followed the first exit sign they could find. It was an emergency staircase that led them downstairs. The murmur now filled the whole floor. In front of them, the corridor seemed to get longer before their eyes.

"There must be fifteen doors along this hall!" protested Alain Rousseau. "We haven't got all night!"

"As far as I know, this floor isn't used, and no one ever comes down here. It's completely vacant." He sniffed the air. "That smell . . . "

"Incense," responded Lucien.

"It's the same as in the basement of the old Protestant church. Come over here!"

He went down another hall that led off to the right from the first one. When he had taken a few steps, he stood in front of a door no different from the others. He took out his weapon, positioned himself to shoot, and motioned to Lucien to open the door when he gave the signal.

A cloud of incense and other aromatic substances wafted out from the room. He went in. The place was dim, with the exception of a few lamps that projected a filtered red glow along the walls. Strange music like the murmurs they had heard earlier floated in the air. When his eyes had got used to the darkness, Dubuc could make out shadowy movements at the back of the room. But from where he was standing, the motions seemed fuzzy and disconnected, as if he was watching a film of his own dream. He felt himself suddenly enveloped in a warm, eerie atmosphere.

"Come forward."

The man's voice was coming from the back of the room. The policeman rubbed his eyes in an unsuccessful effort to identify the speaker. He was about to move forward when he suddenly felt an iron hand grab him from behind and saw a knife blade gleaming overhead.

He fell backwards and a shot echoed through the room. Jules Talbot collapsed to the floor with a loud scream, clutching onto his shoulder with both hands. When Dubuc looked up again, he saw Lucien coming towards them, his revolver still smoking. Alain Rousseau held Talbot down on the floor.

Without a word, Dubuc and Lucien carefully walked towards the small, draped altar at the back of the room. Seven Satanists stood behind it, immobile. They were dressed in black robes with hoods hanging low over their eyes. One of them, taller than the others, had placed a hand on the head of little Marie-Ève Gagnon. The little girl was bound and spread out on the altar, which was covered in a black cloth. Four red candles were burning in the four corners. The smoke from burning incense rose up from several golden urns placed on the floor behind them.

"Good evening, Dr. Rubinsky," Dubuc said.

The other man didn't respond. Dubuc gestured to Lucien to go and untie Marie-Ève. But just as the deputy got close to the altar, a hand rose up and pushed long finger nails deep into his skin. Lucien jumped back, screaming in pain. The flesh of his forearm was cut in long, bloody streaks. His attacker got hold of a lit candle from the altar and jumped on him again, shouting with extraordinary violence. Lucien managed to escape the attack and disarm his opponent. He pulled back the black hood. It was Sophie Ménard.

"Poor Sophie," said Dubuc, as Lucien put handcuffs

around her small wrists as she fought back with obvious rage. "I had a feeling you'd be around tonight. You never stray too far from Marie-Ève, do you?"

The Satanist in the centre of the group approached them and the police officers pulled back his hood too. Dubuc had been right. It was Stanley Rubinsky. The psychiatrist held out both hands towards the policemen.

"It's all over for me," he whispered, overcome with emotion. "J.A. and Conrad gave me a lot of trouble, but I had to get rid of the father and son so I'd be able to take over as leader."

"I've suspected you for quite a while," sighed Dubuc. "After we met in the funeral parlour, you convinced me that Conrad detested J.A. because he had him committed. Then, when you told me he escaped from your hospital the day his father was killed, he became my number one suspect. That's what you wanted, eh?"

Rubinsky nodded his head.

"You were brilliant," continued Dubuc. "Conrad was a good scapegoat for a while. But I eventually realized the poor guy couldn't have killed J.A. His medication made him tremble. The autopsy report from the coroner showed that J.A.'s stab wounds were clean. So I figured out Conrad couldn't have killed his father. Granted, it was too late."

Dubuc motioned towards the policeman from the SQ, who came up and put handcuffs on the psychiatrist.

"After Conrad's death," he continued, "you tried to shift our suspicions away from the cult by implicating Serge Brindle, your farm manager. You made us think he was a real weirdo, according to this nurse he used to date. False! I did my little investigation, you see. No one in your ward ever dated Brindle. The guy was involved in a tussle when he was young and one of his chums is paralyzed for life. When he told us about it he had tears in his eyes."

The police officer took a notebook out of his pocket and leafed through it.

"In any case, Dr. Rubinsky, I've got enough to go on. I know that J.A.'s murderer and Conrad's is one and the same. But it isn't you."

The psychiatrist gasped. "Gosh! What more do you need, Dubuc? A third murder?"

"How generous of you to offer, Doc. But I know very well who you're trying to protect. You are up to your neck in the organization. I don't have a motive yet, so I can't accuse you of murdering J.A., but the evidence is pretty convincing. It's obvious that you were there when J.A. and Conrad Bussières were killed."

Lucien looked at his boss and tried to figure out where he was going.

"So who then?"

Another member of the cult came up to Stanley Rubinsky and pulled down the black hood. It was Marguerita Bussières. J.A.'s widow broke the tension that reigned over the smoky room by clapping her hands vigorously.

"Bravo! Good show! We have our own Hercule Poirot." she shouted.

"Calm down!" Dubuc ordered. "You were the one who had the most to gain from J.A.'s and Conrad's deaths. Greed is always a motive we have to consider. I was tearing my hair out for days, trying to figure it out: Why at the cemetery? Isn't that an odd place to kill someone? A murder like J.A.'s is planned for quite a while ahead of time, especially in a morbid place like this. And whoever planned the murder had to know exactly where to find him, where exactly they could hide while they were waiting. Marguerita, you knew very well that your husband went out to see his young mistresses at Motel Roger on Wednesday nights, while you went to see your sister in Sherbrooke. The motel's owner, Thérèse Roger, confirmed my suspicions that J.A. was a regular. You probably also knew – maybe you snuck out and followed him some nights – that he always took the short cut through the cemetery to get home, because his chauffeur didn't wait for him. When you come right down to it, the graveyard was the perfect place to kill him. It's dark, remote, and it was the only time J.A.'s chauffeur wasn't around. He followed him everywhere else."

Marguerita Bussières, who had calmed down now, muttered in a monotone: "What proof do you have that . . . ?"

The policeman reached into his pocket, pulled out a half-chewed cigarillo and flashed it under her nose. "This. This proof. It's a little cigar from Havana. Top-notch. A supplier from Montréal assured me that J.A. was the only customer he had from this area. It was lying in the grass, soaking wet, when I picked it up the morning after your husband's murder. I thought he'd probably dropped it when he realized he was being followed. It took me a long time to figure out what it really meant. In your living room, Marguerita."

The widow looked astonished. "At my place?"

"Yes, indeed! One morning when I paid you a visit I knocked over an ashtray. I have to confess: it wasn't really an accident. The ashes spilled all over your nice Persian carpet. You remember? I had made sure I got there early, before the housekeeper. So while you were looking for a cloth, I had a quick peak through the cigarette butts on the carpet. One of them was a cigarillo, identical to the one I'd picked up in the cemetery the night of the murder. J.A.'s? Well, no, obviously, he couldn't have been the one smoking it. This was several days after his death, and your housekeeper would have had lots of time to clean out the ashtrays. When I looked at it more closely, I noticed that there were lipstick marks on the end. Just like the one from the cemetery. It's only after I got this cigar butt from your living room that I realized what a treasure I'd discovered in the graveyard. You see, J.A. wasn't the only one who smoked expensive Cuban cigarillos. The other one who did was a woman, and she had to have been in the cemetery the night of the murder of J.A. Bussières."

Stupefied, the widow looked at the two cigarillo butts lying in the palm of the policeman's hand.

"I smoke them once in a while, yes. They calm my nerves. I did the night before your visit because I had a feeling you'd be questioning me. I couldn't settle down. I guess I should have given up that awful habit after my husband's death." She shook her head slowly with a disappointed look on her face. "You're implicating me in the murder because of a simple cigarillo."

"I'm arresting you as an accomplice in your husband's murder, Marguerita. But unless I'm mistaken, you didn't actually kill him."

She shrugged her shoulders. She looked as though she was resigned to whatever explanations the police chief was about to give.

"Your high heels, Marguerita!"

The widow lowered her head and the attention of the entire group was suddenly drawn to her pumps.

"How tall are you?" asked Dubuc, point-blank.

Her only response was to look offended.

"Never mind," continued Dubuc. "You're pretty short, wouldn't you agree? Let's say you're around five feet tall. Your high heels give you a few centimetres more. Now I have nothing against a woman being coquettish. I can give you that. But you're obsessed with it. I got my proof of it when I dropped in on you very early one morning. You were still in your bathrobe, but you already had your heels on. So I'd say chances are pretty good that you were wearing them when you went to the cemetery."

The widow was mute. Dubuc continued: "The day after the murder, it was the way you walked that struck me. There you were, tears in your eyes, coming into the cemetery. You were tiptoeing, like a little mouse. Because of those incredibly high heels on your feel. The coroner's report revealed that J.A. was chased by his murderer before falling victim to the crime. But with those shoes, my dear Marguerita, it would have been impossible to run after him, even with the best intentions in the world! The night of the murder, you certainly had a sufficient motive to kill your husband, but it wasn't you who did it."

Lucien turned to Dubuc. He was obviously exasperated by the way the police chief was keeping everyone waiting.

Chapter 15

Roméo Dubuc was cackling with satisfaction.

"Ah, Lucien. Patience, Old Boy. I won't keep you in suspense much longer, but I do have to put all the pieces of the puzzle in place. I'm almost finished."

He turned to the grocer who was sitting, motionless, on the ground behind him.

"What kept me from suspecting that the cult could be involved in the murders, for a long time, was the violent temper that Jules has."

Responding to a gesture from Dubuc, Alain Rousseau, the policeman, stood the grocer up on his feet and took him over to where the other Satanists were standing.

"He made the perfect suspect!" Dubuc said. "The guy had every reason in the world to want to kill J.A.! He was hovering around his daughter Pauline. So much so that he threatened to kill him. In front of people."

Dubuc turned towards Talbot and squeezed one of his enormous biceps. "Physically, you certainly have the advantage. You're as strong as Rambo, skilled with a knife, and your alibi the night of the murder wasn't too solid. I spent quite a few nights tossing and turning before I took you off my list of suspects. I had to, though. Dr. Moreau informed me that J.A. Bussières must have had to run to get away from his murderer, because of the low levels of ATP in his organism. So you couldn't have done it. How could a lame man like you, Jules, a veteran of the Canadian Armed Forces, wounded by a stray bullet, have been able to catch J.A. and kill him? So I had to accept the evidence. It was impossible. And I haven't even got to your hands."

Roméo Dubuc approached Talbot and held up one of

his hands. "Strong, muscular, like a farmer's hands, Jules. The palms are calloused, which proves that you spend a good part of your day lugging crates around your grocery store."

The chief's explanations seemed to be going over Talbot's head now.

"On my first visit to the grocery store you got pretty upset, talking about Bussières and Pauline. Remember that? You grabbed a nail file, which you had plunged into your desk earlier. In rage. That made me think to look at your nails, which were short and neatly trimmed. I wondered if the murderer could have so horribly disfigured the victim if he had nails like yours. Unlikely. So you couldn't have murdered J.A. And yet you were at the cemetery the night of the murder, Jules. Yes, indeed, you were there."

"I didn't kill J.A. It's good to finally hear that!" Jules Talbot said in a voice rough with emotion. "As far as the rest of it goes, well, I didn't have anything to do with it."

"Not so fast!" retorted Dubuc. "It's your daughter Pauline that put me on the trail. Not that she wanted to. If you had seen her at the factory, that poor girl . . . She was a pitiful sight to be seen, when she found out the police knew she'd slept with J.A. the night of the murder. Your little Pauline has a holy terror of you, Jules. She told me that if she ever got home five minutes late she was in big trouble. What got me was that, the night of the murder, Pauline had come home an hour late, and nothing happened to her. No argument, no punishment. I took note of that in my book. Pauline told me: "I ran like an idiot all the way home in the pouring rain, and went straight to bed." According to my information, it was nearly eleven o'clock. So why didn't you yell at her that night, Jules? Well, because you weren't at home, and neither was your wife, when Pauline got in. You were at the cemetery with the others."

With these words, Dubuc went up to one of the Satanists, who seemed to be trying to control desperate sobs. Dubuc pulled on the hood. It was Lorraine Talbot.

The loud arrival of Sergeant Trépanier of the SQ and his men, who had been contacted by radio, disrupted the atmosphere of the smoke-filled room. Trépanier spread his eight officers around the room and they waited for their orders. After making sure none of the suspects were armed, Trépanier signalled to his men to step back a bit. Dubuc went towards the altar and brusquely pulled off another Satanist's hood. It was Jerry Ménard. The police officer showed no sign of surprise. He turned towards the other Satanists.

"I wondered for a long time why Jerry had decided to come back to Chesterville after being in exile for so many years. I couldn't come up with a logical explanation. Except money. J.A. had agreed to lend you a hundred and fifty thousand bucks, without interest, for ten years, so that you could fix up the Greluche. In return, you were supposed to do him some 'favours,' right, Jerry?"

"I don't know what you're talking about," Jerry replied with a tone of mockery.

"If you knew J.A. the way I did, you'd know very well that the guy always wanted something in return for a favour. And this time he lent you a big sum of money without interest, to fix up the Greluche of course, but also so you'd come back to Chesterville to join the cult. With your daughter."

"I just wanted to get into business," retorted Jerry.

Roméo Dubuc burst out laughing when he heard this. "Yes, I imagine. Unfortunately, I don't think you had any choice, Jerry. You were getting over a serious depression, your finances were down to nothing, and J.A.'s offer couldn't have come a better time. You jumped at the chance like a famished dog someone tosses a bone to."

"Let's say J.A. did convince me to join the cult. That doesn't prove I killed him!" argued Ménard.

"But the temptation must have been pretty strong. J.A. didn't only lend you a hundred and fifty thousand bucks, without interest, but the loan was forgiven if he happened to die. Bussières signed that rather unusual clause on the condition that you supplied him regularly with girls. You're the one who told me that. It was the kind of contract that gave you a pretty good motive to kill him."

Dubuc went up to Jerry Ménard and grabbed his left hand.

"You weren't armed that night, Jerry. But when I cornered you in the restroom of the Esso garage the other night, I noticed that you were left-handed."

Ménard shrugged his shoulders. He didn't understand.

"Seeing me there gave you such a fright that you instinctively reached for your piece by slipping your left hand inside your jacket. That night, I realized that you weren't the murderer I was looking for. According to the coroner, J.A.'s murderer had to be right-handed, according to the angle at which the blade penetrated the body. In spite of everything, I still had the feeling that Sophie and you were at the cemetery the night of the murder. I just had to prove it."

"I didn't kill J.A. And I wasn't at the cemetery either."

"When you fell in the swamp while we were searching for Marie-Ève and your daughter, your shoes sank into the mud and I was the one who got them out," continued Dubuc. "I couldn't help but notice that your fine Italian leather shoes were a bit the worse for wear that day. They were especially worn on the right heel."

"It's normal for shoes to get worn down, isn't it?" said Ménard.

"Well, sure. But not behind the heel. The only other

person who had that habit, as far as I know, was J.A. Bussières. He lit his Cuban cigarillos by rubbing wooden matches behind his right heel, and in the long run that wore them down. But you don't smoke. And, on top of it, you're left-handed. Where did that mark on the back of your right heel come from, Jerry?"

Jerry hesitated a moment too long.

"I'll tell you where. You're strutting around in J.A.'s shoes. You took them from him in the cemetery the night of the murder. We looked everywhere for his shoes, near the corpse, around the graveyard. Your eyes must have popped out of your head when you thought about it, Jerry. You couldn't stop yourself from taking those beautiful Italian leather shoes off the corpse. You'll be accused of being an accomplice in the murder."

Dubuc gestured to the SQ officer, who put handcuffs on the owner of the Greluche. Then the police chief headed towards the last Satanist who still wore a hood, and pulled it down. What he saw made him flinch. It was Liette Bardois. It took the police chief a long, tense moment to recover his composure. His voice trembled with emotion.

"Until the very last moment, I kept believing that you and André had nothing to do with this cult, Liette. But your presence here tonight has taken away the last of my illusions."

He slipped his hand around Liette Bardois's neck and his fingers found a delicate chain, from which a charm hung. It was the black cat. Confronted with a reality that he had tried to avoid since the death of his own son, Roméo Dubuc fell to his knees and put his head down on the ground. He stayed in this position for several minutes. The sobs he tried to stifle broke through the heavy silence every few seconds. Silent tension reigned over the smoky room. Finally, he pulled himself up on his feet, still fighting the deep despair that had taken hold of him. He turned towards a policeman and motioned to him to take Liette Bardois away immediately.

Lucien, who had followed the reasoning of his boss quite well up until now, turned towards Sophie.

"Don't tell me that it's her . . . "

"I had a really hard time convincing myself that Sophie might have murdered J.A. Bussières and Conrad with the complicity of the cult. After all, who would suspect a pretty little blond girl with an angelic face like hers? My first suspects were, naturally, adults. But after a while I got to the point where I had to face the evidence. Everything leans in the right direction to suggest that it was a child who actually killed J.A. and his son."

"Get serious!" interrupted Stan Rubinsky with a look of disdain. "You won't get a jury to buy that one."

"You're right, Doctor," agreed Dubuc. "In the eyes of the community, a ten-year-old girl is more often a victim than a criminal. Much more often. I admit the toughest thing for me was to convince myself that a little girl could commit murder in cold blood. My second question was why anyone would kill two people at an age when most girls are more interested in playing with dolls."

"What tangible proof do you have?" Rubinsky asked with interest. "This little girl is the very portrait of innocence!"

Dubuc's only response was to take Sophie's two hands and turn them towards the psychiatrist.

"Look at these hands, Doctor. They're messy, always stained by the wildflowers Sophie picks, plucks apart and tosses around her wherever she goes, all day long. I had already noticed the yellow stains on the handle of the knife we found in the warehouse, as well as on the rope that was used to hang Conrad. And I also wondered why in the world J.A. Bussières's hand was clutching a wild daisy when he was found. On his way down to the ground, J.A. must have managed to grab a daisy that Sophie probably had in her hair. Several days later, Sophie repeated the same routine, tossing daisy petals all over the barn behind the hospital, around Conrad's corpse. This coincidence seemed pretty bizarre. I figured it couldn't just be chance. When I got back to the office, I examined the rope Conrad had supposedly used to commit suicide and discovered, as you've probably guessed, yellow stains on it. It seemed plausible that Sophie was involved in the murders of J.A. and Conrad."

"My daughter was just following me!" cried out Jerry Ménard, trying to repress his tears. "Sophie didn't kill anyone! She didn't!"

Roméo Dubuc let his hands fall to his side in a gesture of helplessness.

"I'd really like to believe you, Jerry. But unless I've made a terrible error, all the other suspects who had a good reason to kill J.A. and Conrad couldn't have done it. They were just hanging around to watch. It must have been Sophie who actually carried out the murders."

Jerry struggled with his rage, but Stan Rubinsky calmed him down with a nod of his head. He turned towards the chief with a weary air.

"You should know that, in the last six months of his life, J.A. Bussières had become a horribly cruel man. A real monster. At the beginning, three years ago, the Cult of the Cat was just entertainment. I had heard about the activities of the American cult, and I'm the one who recruited some members in Chesterville. Every week, when we met, we read passages from the Satanic Bible and burned red candles. It was really quite harmless. That's all we wanted. Our meetings were held in secret in the basements of some members' homes. But, little by little, things started to change. We started getting bolder. Some of the members of our group found out that the American cult sacrificed small animals to Satan, the King of Hell, and wanted to imitate them. That's about the time I convinced J.A. Bussières and Marguerita to join our group. Since J.A. wasn't the kind of man who did things by halves, the cult got even bolder. We started catching pet cats and offering them as a sacrifice to Satan in secret places in Chesterville, and drinking their blood."

"I imagine the members of the cult took drugs during these rituals?" asked Dubuc.

"Of course!" replied Stanley Rubinsky. "Nobody who was in their right mind would drink blood and urine from alley cats unless they were under some kind of hallucinogenic. As a doctor, I was the one who could supply members of the cult with psychotropic substances. Usually it was marijuana and sometimes LSD. It was pretty easy because I had access to the pharmacy in the hospital. But as time went on, things got worse."

"What do you mean?"

"Well, the cult members had to take stronger doses of drugs each time to get through the rituals, because J.A. was going farther and farther during the Black Mass ceremonies. After sacrificing cats, it was farm animals, especially dairy cows and heifers. But it was when little Sophie Ménard arrived that the sexual assaults really started, about six months ago."

"What?" Dubuc was incredulous.

"Everyone could tell that J.A. was interested in Sophie. I'd say he was obsessed with her. Jerry was worried but nobody dared question J.A.'s supreme authority. After all, he was the Grand Chingon of the cult. And it was J.A. who had introduced the idea of symbolically offering a young virgin to Satan during the Black Mass."

Rubinsky turned towards Marie-Ève.

"As you know, we continued this 'symbolic' practice

even after the death of J.A., but without hurting this little girl. Unfortunately, we can't say the same for poor Sophie. It was too late for her."

"What do you mean 'too late'?" insisted Dubuc.

"After a while, J.A. started giving presents to Sophie, kissing her and fondling her more and more openly, in front of all the other members. Right up to the day he decided to make her Satan's bride. It's a very skilful way of abusing someone sexually during satanic rituals. Sophie was dressed in a wedding dress and raped by J.A., regularly, under the pretext of offering her purity and innocence to Satan."

"And your gang of imbeciles let it happen?" growled Dubuc.

"Listen, Chief Dubuc, you have to understand," Stan Rubinsky answered calmly. "At that stage of a satanic ceremony most of the members have already collapsed on the ground, stoned out of their skulls. And besides, J.A. asked me every time to slip some drugs into everyone's drinks. It weakened the willpower of all the members and lasted several hours. So it wasn't hard at all to convince them that what he was doing to Sophie was all right. And so was everything else."

"Were you drugged too, like the others?"

"No," replied the psychiatrist. "Since I was in charge of preparing the drugs, I needed to keep my wits about me most of the time. I already told you about my past, during the Vietnam war, when I was in the American army. I was the camp medic, and I was trained to ease the suffering of wounded and mutilated soldiers. I saw unspeakable horrors. I'm afraid they hardened my heart and soul."

"Enough that you could close your eyes to the disgusting horrors of J.A.'s behaviour!" shouted Dubuc.

"I admit that during the satanic rituals, J.A. had an enormous control over everyone. He dominated them completely, and me too," continued Stan Rubinsky. "He was the supreme head of the cult and we accepted him body and soul. After a while, though, we started questioning his authority. Some of us found the situation had become intolerable, totally repulsive. J.A. was even talking about kidnapping other little girls from nearby villages to sexually abuse them during the rituals. That's when the members of the cult finally decided we had to put a stop to it."

"In other words, you orchestrated the murder of J.A. in the cemetery together?" suggested Roméo Dubuc.

"In a way, yes," said Rubinsky. "I can tell you that Bussières's murder was planned down to the last second, with the precision of a Swiss watch. In the mind of the members of the cult, Sophie needed to symbolically liberate herself from the control J.A. had over her by stabbing him, two ritual blows with a knife. To make that work, we helped her in the cemetery. Sophie chased J.A. over to his family plot, while Jules and Jerry held him down so that she could stab him in the heart. It wasn't easy, because J.A. put up a fight. He was going nuts. Your investigation was very well done, Chief Dubuc, because you were right about us all being there at the cemetery. But everything was supposed to be taken care of after J.A.'s murder."

"But unfortunately the cult also decided to kill Conrad?"

"It was a tragic error. No one could have predicted what a liberating effect killing J.A. Bussières would have on Sophie. The little girl refused to go home after the murder. She stayed in the cemetery half the night, rolling around in the grass, meowing with pleasure like a cat near J.A.'s corpse."

"And disfiguring him with her nails?"

"I'm afraid so," replied Rubinsky, lowering his head.

"But why Conrad?" asked Dubuc.

The psychiatrist shrugged his shoulders. "Who can pretend

to understand the mental state of a little girl as troubled as Sophie? I sure can't. One thing is for sure. The little girl realized pretty quickly what a salvation the murder of J.A. Bussières was for her, and she probably thought the murder of another member of the Bussières family, like Conrad, would have the same effect on her. It all happened as though J.A.'s murder induced a state of euphoria in Sophie that she wanted instinctively to maintain, as though that pleasure became an addiction for her."

"So the cult didn't plan Conrad's murder?"

"Not at all. Sophie did it all on her own. The day of the murder, she asked me to go with her to the barn of the hospital. I forget why. Anyway, I agreed. We hid out for over an hour until Conrad came to get the hay in. Because I was his doctor, he didn't suspect anything when I gave him enough medicine to put a horse out, as the coroner so carefully showed. In spite of that, though, Conrad struggled when Sophie tried to put a rope around his neck. I admit I panicked at the thought of Conrad being able to identify us as being his assailants, because that meant everyone would make an immediate connection with the cult. Without really thinking, I helped Sophie strangle Conrad with a wire before dangling his corpse at the end of a rope to make everyone think it was suicide."

"It all sounds plausible," Dubuc commented, noting that Sophie could have murdered Conrad because she was under observation at the hospital during the same period of time.

The policeman asked Lucien to take Sophie out. Then he turned to the psychiatrist.

"Dr. Rubinsky, you didn't hesitate to help this little girl murder two people. And a moment ago, you protected her when you said you were the murderer. Why would you sacrifice yourself for her?" Dubuc asked, obviously perplexed.

The psychiatrist turned to the other members of the cult and sighed before he answered.

"I don't know really. Maybe because of the horrific events we went through together. During the satanic rituals we were all helpless to intervene. But I want you to know I would do anything in my power to help this little girl. Whatever I can. And I think everyone in the cult that is here tonight would tell you the same thing.

With a signal from Chief Dubuc, the policemen posted around the room moved forward to take away the other members of the Cult of the Cat.

★

Catherine Gagnon rushed towards her daughter when the procession of policemen and prisoners finally paraded out of the hospital.

"Marie-Ève! Oh, dear Lord!"

She crouched on one knee and pulled her daughter close to her, holding her wet cheek against her daughter's for a moment.

Then Catherine raised her face towards Dubuc. "Did they . . . ?"

Dubuc shook his head, and leaned down towards the little girl himself. "I don't think so. They tied Marie-Ève to the altar to offer her as a sacrifice to Satan, but it had become a symbolic practice after J.A.'s death. According to Rubinsky, the cult had had enough of the sexual assaults that your uncle had inflicted on Sophie Ménard. They planned his murder in the cemetery together, and let Sophie have the privilege of stabbing him to death."

"How is she doing?" asked Catherine.

"In Dr. Rubinsky's own opinion, she's a child who will be seriously disturbed until the end of her days. You're the one who was right the other night, when you insisted on questioning her. We'll have to see what the court decides, but a ten-year-old girl who commits two murders and gets such pleasure out of doing it needs to be treated in an institution. Not to mention that the sequels of sexual abuse aren't going to disappear overnight. As for Marie-Ève . . . "

"What about Marie-Ève?" Catherine asked nervously.

"I was just going to suggest that you have her undergo a physical and psychological examination once you get back to Vermont. After all, Rubinsky did chloroform her and lock her up in the dark for nearly three days in the damp cellar of the hospital for which he was the only one who had a key."

"I'll do it as soon as we get home."

"Are you leaving soon?"

"Tomorrow, around noon. I don't think that we have anything more to do around here."

*

At ten o'clock the next morning, Catherine, Marie-Ève and Barbara slowly walked down the steps of the police station. When he saw them, Chief Dubuc went to meet them and pulled them in for a hug. "On your way then?"

"We came to say good bye to you and Lucien."

"You know, I'm really sorry about your Aunt Marguerita," said Dubuc, feeling rather awkward.

"It's sad, I know, but I suppose she has to pay for her mistakes like everyone else."

"Especially since the cult is involved in two murders as well as the attempt to poison Toto Grimaldi. We can't simply wipe that kind of thing off the record. It will probably mean several years of prison for everyone involved."

"And how about Toto? How is he?"

"Oh, Antonio will get through it. Lucien went to the hospital to see him early this morning. It seems that the first thing Toto saw when he opened his eyes was his wife telling him off! "

They laughed heartily.

"Do you think the arrests will put the Cult of the Cat out of commission for good in Chesterville?" Catherine asked, hugging Marie-Ève close.

"Who knows? Cults are a bizarre phenomenon. They are pretty seductive. The news is out and I guarantee that we'll have as many reporters as telephone poles in Chesterville within the next few days. But I am convinced that we dealt a pretty hard blow to the local organization."

As though attempting to ward off these dark thoughts, the policeman got up, walked over to a box set on a chair and came back, holding a little ball of black and white fur in his hands. He held it out to Marie-Ève.

"Here, little one. This is for you."

"A kitty!" exclaimed Marie-Ève, her eyes suddenly sparkling with joy.

"To help her get over Coconut's death," Dubuc whispered to Catherine.

"What are you going to name it?" asked Catherine, stroking the kitten herself.

Marie-Ève raised the kitten up to her face and looked straight into its eyes.

"I'm going to call it Moon."

"Moon? That's an interesting name for a cat," commented the police chief.

"It's because cats like to come out at night," replied Marie-Ève with a serious look on her face.

Catherine said her good-byes to Chief Dubuc and to Lucien.

She helped her daughter and Barbara into the car,

slipped behind the steering wheel and drove for several kilometres. The day was sunny and the heat started to crawl over them as the afternoon went on. She slowed down at the sight of a snack bar at the side of the road.

"Would you like to have something to drink, Girls?"

"Not me," replied Marie-Ève, stroking her cat. "I want to stay here with Moon."

Catherine headed for the snack bar with Barbara at her side. But when they got back a few moments later, Marie-Ève had disappeared. Catherine looked around. Nobody.

"Marie-Ève!"

Her heart pounding in her chest, she circled the snack bar. No luck. Then she wove her way through the dozen parked cars. A woman pointed in the direction of the woods behind the parking lot.

"I saw a little girl go that way with her cat."

Catherine and Barbara ran in the direction she was pointing. After crossing a little bridge over a creek, they saw Marie-Ève standing at the edge of the forest, in the middle of a clump of tall weeds. The little girl was motionless, staring at the ground.

"You said you'd stay in the Jeep! Where is your kitten?"

She pointed towards the forest.

"He got away. He went far, far away, Mama."

"Come with me. We'll go find him."

Catherine took Marie-Ève's hand and they walked together into the woods. They hadn't gone more than twenty steps before Catherine noticed a pool of blood on the narrow path. She knelt down and saw the cat, dead, crushed by a large, flat rock.

"Oooooh, what's happened here . . . ?"

She turned to her daughter.

Marie-Ève was grinning.

Printed in October 2006
at Gauvin Press, Gatineau, Québec